BRUBAKER

Tough, shrewd, brave, and incorruptible—
and determined to change Wakefield
Prison . . .

BRUBAKER

Posing as a prisoner, he learns firsthand
the shocking truth about a savage, brutal
system that turns human beings into
slaves . . .

BRUBAKER

The crusading prison warden who finds
himself up against a violent backwoods
town, an indifferent prison board, a
corrupt senator—and even a woman he
thought he could trust—as he struggles to
bring some humanity to a hell on earth . . .

BRUBAKER

If he has to put them all behind bars to
change Wakefield Prison, he plans to do it.

TWENTIETH CENTURY-FOX PRESENTS

A TED MANN—RON SILVERMAN PRODUCTION

A STUART ROSENBERG FILM

ROBERT REDFORD

IN

BRUBAKER

YAPHET KOTTO

JANE ALEXANDER

MURRAY HAMILTON

DAVID KEITH

and

TIM McINTIRE as Huey

Executive Producer
TED MANN

Produced by
RON SILVERMAN

Directed by
STUART ROSENBERG

Screenplay by
W. D. RICHTER

Story by
W. D. RICHTER and ARTHUR ROSS

Music by
LALO SCHIFRIN

COLOR BY DeLUXE (R)

BRUBAKER

**Novelization by
WILLIAM HARRISON**

**based on the screenplay by
W. D. RICHTER**

BALLANTINE BOOKS • NEW YORK

Library of Congress Catalog Card Number: 80-66170

ISBN 0-345-29134-4

Manufactured in the United States of America

First Edition: July 1980

1

THE city sat in the bend of a quiet river; its buildings gray in the early morning light, smoke and mist hovering around the docks where barges and riverboats waited, its factories and traffic not yet alive. There were distant noises though: the hard metallic sound of a steel door somewhere, iron sliding across iron, and the sound, too, of an old bus engine wheezing uphill.

The bus bore the letters WAKEFIELD PRISON FARM on its drab gray side. Slowly, its gears grinding, the bus made its way through the streets. The pavements glistened with last night's cold rain. The sky overhead sat low and promised another forlorn day of winter.

At the county jail doors clanged open and several prisoners in civilian clothes were ushered outside as the bus squealed to a halt. Two deputies, indolent and seemingly unconcerned, flanked the prisoners and held their shotguns casually in the crooks of their arms. One of them picked at his teeth with his finger, looked up at the cold sky and shivered. As the doors of the bus opened, the prisoners climbed inside, one by one, without instruction, and took their seats. Beside the driver, facing the new passengers, was a uniformed guard who leveled another shotgun in their direction. Nobody spoke. Although this trip was new to the prisoners, they had been instructed to keep quiet, so the movements looked practiced and orderly.

Soon the bus moved through the city streets again, its occupants gazing out the wire mesh windows. The downtown section of this modest river city soon passed away and neighborhoods moved before the prisoners'

1

eyes—cars parked at the curbs, children's tricycles in the yards, trees and darkened windows. The normalcies of life out there seemed far away to the men, the houses forbidding and dark, the town suddenly empty. Then they were in the countryside: a flat delta region where the sky opened up long horizons of open fields. Again, they watched this flat landscape as if in a stupor. Only one of the prisoners seemed to be observant and fully awake.

Both black and white men occupied the rear of the prison bus. Their dress was varied and sad, tattered sweaters and jackets, an occasional sport coat out of season with the winter weather, the disparate clothing of city boys and rural types who were down and out.

Only one of them—the observant one, who now studied the slumping form of the Transfer Man with his menacing shotgun—wore a tie, but it was loosened. Even so, he looked oddly out of place, less passive somehow and more cleverly attentive than the driver, the guard, or his fellow prisoners. His name was Henry Brubaker, but he wasn't going to prison as that. This man was known to the others as "Stan Collins."

Across the aisle sat Frank Zaranska, who wore the most garish outfit of all the prisoners, shiny white plastic shoes and red socks, a loud striped sport coat made of cheap doubleknit, a wide-open collar. He looked as though he had just been imported from Miami for this doleful journey through the hick countryside. Nervous, he tried to whistle, but the noise that came from his lips was tuneless and pathetic. The young man beside Zaranska was trying even harder to appear tough and unconcerned, but Glenn Elwood's surly self-confidence was wasted on everyone who watched him except Brubaker. The men were all uneasy, caved in on themselves, already alone and isolated from those separate worlds from which they had come.

The bad brakes began to squeal. Everyone looked up toward the driver who was stopping the bus in the middle of nowhere.

"Lookee here," the armed Transfer Man said, and the prisoners shifted slightly so that they could view the small patch of woods alongside the country highway. A dirt trail led off into the woods and two men, armed with shotguns, were dragging the body of a third man toward the bus. All three were dressed in prison clothes, those unmistakable gray fatigues.

Then everyone on the bus saw clearly that the man being dragged had been shot. The back of his shirt had been riddled with buckshot and was soaked red with blood.

"Who the hell are they?" Glenn Elwood asked.

"Convicts," Zaranska answered. "All three of them, baby, same as us. Wakefield prisoners."

As they reached the highway beside the bus, one of the men pumped his shotgun in the air. A sign of greeting. A victory salute.

The bus driver opened the door and the Transfer Man, no longer paying his charges on the bus much attention, broke into laughter.

"What you boys got?" the Transfer Man asked loudly.

"Man with a little rabbit in him," said the rankman who had been waving his gun.

Far off in the woods came the sounds of distant chainsaws. The heavy odor of exhaust filled the bus.

"Throw him on," the Transfer Man said.

"We'll give him a ride with these new boys," the driver added, and those who handled the wounded man all laughed together.

Brubaker studied the two men out beside the road. The wounded man slumped in the arms of a convict in a black watch cap, a man Brubaker would later know as Eddie Caldwell. There was little in either man's face except the solemn impassive stare of pain, so that both hunter and hunted, dressed alike, both cold, both worn out, were much the same.

The Transfer Man and the other rankman were still laughing as the wounded man was brought inside the bus and dropped down in the aisle. All the riders shifted and tried to get a better view. Eddie Caldwell, his watch cap pulled down hard around his ears for warmth, swung himself inside the bus too.

"You guys lookin' to get you a parole?" the driver asked, grinning at his new passengers.

Brubaker watched and listened as if he didn't know what all this meant.

For a moment, the wounded man's eyes fluttered open.

"He ain't gonna make it," someone said.

"Aw, he ain't shot bad," Eddie Caldwell claimed.

The bus lurched forward again. As it moved on, Brubaker glanced out the window and watched the remaining rankman disappear back into the treeline. The echo of those distant chainsaws receded as the bus picked up speed once more. Prison property was nowhere near, Brubaker knew, but prisoners were out there working for someone; it was an old scheme in these parts, the tradition and the system.

Soon they rolled into a small town. Stores and filling stations. A white clapboard church. Pickup trucks beneath the barren trees.

On the far side of town they came to a roadhouse, Pinky's Cafe Bar. The bus driver honked the horn as they passed by.

Then they turned off the county highway and onto a winding serpentine strip of asphalt which led back toward the river. When Brubaker saw a line of rank-men working the dead stubble of a distant field, he knew they had come onto prison land. Wakefield Farm was an immensity of space from the highway to the levee, thousands of acres of crops, separate truck gardens, stands of woodland, ponds, marshes. It was the largest single farm in the state. Men had spent thirty-year sentences here and had never seen it all; many knew of isolated shacks, levee houses, distant corners, hiding spots and secret glades without having actually been to them. There were legends and tales, men and myths, and the farm, grim and forbidding on this winter day, seemed large enough to hold them all.

Soon the main buildings were in sight. These were low, weathered structures of blackened brick. Fences —most of them in need of mending—ran everywhere like a maze.

The bus moved inside the compound through the sallyport gate. Rain had left puddles of gray water and a quagmire of mud before the main building, so that was precisely where they stopped.

"Come on, up, up, you done hit bottom," the Transfer Man told them, waving the barrel of his gun toward the door of the bus. Slowly they then began to file out.

Eddie Caldwell, his watch cap down over his ears, his shotgun cradled in his arm, started an unhurried walk to the infirmary, leaving his victim, shot and bleeding, down in the aisle of the bus so that the new prisoners had to step over him as they emerged.

Brubaker paused above the wounded man before leaving the bus. The man was still breathing, still alive.

Then the cold outdoors again.

An immense black trusty stood before them in a dark rain slicker. He was armed with a sawed-off shotgun which had a stock carved in the shape of a pistol grip.

"Shut you lips and keep moving," he told the arrivals. "You don' wanta piss me off 'fore lunch."

The big black was Dickie Coombes. He herded them along by waving the sawed-off shotgun and grunting, so it seemed in this first impression that he was half animal, half machine; that black slicker and blue-black gun barrel conveyed his mechanical, unfeeling regard for them all.

Brubaker still watched the infirmary across the way. Eddie Caldwell had stopped to light a cigarette and was taking his time. The man on the bus had a good chance of bleeding to death before getting help. Reluctant to go inside and forget the wounded man, Brubaker paused just long enough so that Coombes shot him a special glance. Move on, it told him, and he did.

The last man inside Wakefield barracks was Zaranska. Pulling his pants up by the crotch, he tried to keep his cuffs and white plastic shoes as clean as possible, and was doing a kind of tiptoe dance toward the door when Coombes swatted him with the gun barrel.

The corridor of the main building was wide and poorly lighted. Some twenty feet across, it had stations where desks and chairs were clustered. Down at the end of the corridor was the mess hall. The main barracks was two flights above this central corridor—huge rooms thronged with bunks and men, overcrowded and wild. One flight up, off a main lounge area, the trusties lived in small separate rooms. On the main floor, too, were the barber shop, and the photo room where Brubaker now stood getting his face and profile recorded. The lights inside that little room, not more than a closet, were white hot. He stood holding his ID tag: COLLINS, STAN. A number was assigned him. Sweat poured down his cheek and he felt helpless and herded.

Then he was in the barber shop.

Zaranska was settling into his chair with a smile on his face, but Brubaker could see that the two trusty barbers had little conversation or humor with all this.

"Just a lil' off around the ears," Zaranska said expansively.

"Costs five to get a regular haircut," the trusty barber said to him, as if reciting. "Two only buys you a crewcut. Or I shave you fuckin' head like the captain wants it—for free."

"Shit," Zaranska said, counting his small roll of one dollar bills. "Better save all this for a bed. I hear I gotta pay for that once I get inside the goddamn barracks."

"You gonna lose your hair then, asshole, an' maybe a ear with it," the trusty said, and he waved the clippers in the air.

Glenn Elwood, the tough kid, some of his spunk already gone, slipped out of the next barber chair and looked at himself in the cracked, greenish mirror. He was bald and shiny. The slightest wince creased his eyes, but he covered his disappointment.

Brubaker was next.

"What'll it be for you?" the trusty barber asked him.

"Leave the ears," he answered.

Eddie Caldwell was passing in the corridor when Glenn Elwood walked out of the shop.

"Hey," Elwood asked him. "What happened to the guy on the bus? The guy you shot?"

Caldwell spun on him quickly, grabbed his crotch with one hand and backed him up against the wall and onto his toes.

"New boy, don't ever talk to me unless I tell you! You hear me?" Caldwell said close to Elwood's face.

Brubaker watched this brief violence from his chair. As the barber started to work, Brubaker produced a five dollar bill from his sock and passed it over his shoulder.

In the next chair, Zaranska's locks were being shaved away and he looked as though he might cry.

In the wardrobe room Brubaker stripped with the others. The exchange of clothes was simple: a new prisoner gave up his clothes and personal effects for worn-out prison pants, shirts and underwear. The prison garments were rags, colorless from years of washing, and the trusties who operated the exchange argued and dealt among themselves for the civilian wear of the newcomers.

"Hey, nice shirt," a trusty said.

"You, gimme that watch," said another, and a new arrival, a kid with a nasty pimple on his chin, obediently slid it off his wrist and passed it across the counter.

"Lookee at this," the trusty said, holding the watch high. "Shit, kid don't know better'n to wear his Bulova to prison!"

Brubaker watched everything, catching on fast. He moved through the wardrobe line, dressing as he went along, then shuffled up the rickety wooden stairs with the other prisoners to the rankmen's barracks on the third floor.

Big Dickie Coombes, still wearing his slicker and looking even meaner, unlocked the door to Barracks C and admitted the line of new arrivals, all of them dressed in rank gray now. The heavy metallic sound of the door sliding open was ominous, so the men entered the barracks with their eyes downcast, looking afraid and lost with their shaved heads and tattered prison clothes.

Huge elephant bars stretching from floor to ceiling shut off the barracks from the corridor. In each barracks was a guard cage, an area encased in heavy wire mesh where a guard could fire a rifle or shotgun into the barracks without fear that a convict could strike back.

Two hundred beds were wedged into a barracks space designed for half that many. The beds were empty because their occupants still labored out in the fields, but even so the clutter gave the room a feeling of chaos and disaster. There were single beds, double bunks, thin worn-out mattresses, dirty sheets, threadbare blankets everywhere. And personal items strewn everywhere: shoes, toothbrushes, magazines, discarded clothes, battered guitars. Above, loose wiring hung from a ceiling which was sagging and cracked. Underfoot, puddles of water had formed as a result of leaks in the ceiling, and a number of beds had been shoved together out of the way of the falling trickles of water.

Near the back wall of the barracks there was a small sitting area, with a big easy chair, stuffing coming out of its sides, three well kept beds and a refrigerator. This was the domain of the building tender, a privileged rankman who enjoyed high status but was not yet a trusty. In Barracks C the tender was Big Wendel. As the new arrivals entered, he came toward them in slow, heavy strides.

At this point, Zaranska made a quick move. He stepped forward and handed Big Wendel two dollars. It was a curious, intelligent gesture—and Brubaker realized that the man in the garish sport coat and white plastic shoes had been here before and knew procedure.

"Where's old Lamar?" Zaranska asked. "He don't have this job no more?"

"What's it look like?" Big Wendel said, folding the money into his shirt pocket. Then, nodding at a rusty double bunk with no mattresses which stood in a shallow pool of water, he added, "That be your bed."

Zaranska looked at his fate with no particular enthusiasm.

"Rest of you grab a blanket and find you a place on the floor," Big Wendel went on. "We talk about beds soon as somebody gets out or dies. Somethin' gonna be for sale after that."

"Where we put our things?" Glenn Elwood asked.

"I give you a fruit crate box. You give me a dollar a week. Nobody messes with your personal shit while you out working. Same for mail. You give me a quarter a letter. Everything comes through me."

Brubaker, looking around, saw a rat scurry across the broken linoleum tile between two bunks.

Big Wendel went on talking. But Brubaker's thoughts had tripped away. It was a place clearly where a man paid in cash for all privilege: eating, sleeping, communicating, staying alive.

Later they sat down to their first meal in the vast dining hall. Again, the hall was guarded by cages. The tables were filthy and pieces of wet plaster had fallen from the sagging ceiling to dot the floor.

Three well-fed servers had filled their plates at the steam tables, but the food was a watery bean soup— colorless, tasteless and awful. As they tried to eat it, a trusty walked around them, sizing them up.

Then the doors at the opposite end of the mess burst open and hundreds of rankmen began to file inside. They counted out for the trusties as they entered. In from the fields, they were exhausted and dirty, and as Brubaker, Zaranska, Elwood and the other arrivals caught sight of them they glimpsed their own futures in this place.

As the rankmen stood in line for the steam tables, they watched the new arrivals in turn.

When Brubaker and the others left the mess hall, they had to surrender the spoons they had been issued at the steam tables. One man, one spoon; permission to leave the mess hall depended on a prisoner tossing his spoon back into a pan under the supervision of a trusty.

"They don' want no weapons made outta them things," Zaranska explained. But, of course, as Brubaker was soon to learn, the barracks were filled with weapons. From the kitchen, from the tool sheds around the farm, from the outside world, Wakefield stored an assortment of knives, guns, knuckles, saps, clubs and icepicks.

That night a rainstorm poured water into the barracks. But the men didn't seem to notice. Radios blared, a man played his harmonica, rankmen exchanged smokes, another prisoner petted his caged raccoon, looking for a little affection from the creature. Many of the prisoners languished in their bunks or walked around wrapped in blankets, wearing old rubber boots for houseshoes, as they waited their turns at the lavatories. Out in the corridor trusties slowly walked by, watching all the activity.

"Ain't no paid guards here, see," Zaranska explained to Brubaker. "Just the trusty system. Prisoners guardin' prisoners. Which is shit, but the state won't pay for professionals."

Brubaker listened and nodded, but Zaranska sensed that Brubaker knew all this.

"You been here before too?" he finally asked.

"Nope, first time."

"You act like you know all I'm tellin' you."

"I heard about this place," Brubaker told him.

"Reckon so," Zaranska said. "Ever'body heard about this place, but you gotta see it to believe it. We got ourselves a fuckin' chicken coop here."

In the lavatory—a facility meant for twenty men, but used by fifty at a time—there was no privacy. Toilets lined one wall, sitting side by side, and men relieved their bladders and bowels while in the company of others. As Brubaker reached for a bar of soap on the floor of the communal showers, a big black man grabbed it away.

"Buy you own," said the black man.

The talk in the showers was all about the women's compound which stood in a grove of cottonwood trees not far from the warden's house on the other side of the farm. The women—there were about thirty female prisoners—worked almost exclusively at sewing machines in a big room overlooking the river. The men in the lavatory discussed the girls, most of whom were prostitutes, they said, and schemed on ways to meet them at the infirmary. There was also talk of shantytown and the closet—things Brubaker determined to learn more about. A lot of the fights, escapes and payoffs in the barracks, he soon learned, concerned ways of meeting the women prisoners at various rendezvous spots on the farm.

When an older rankman dropped his soap in the shower, he told one of the new arrivals, the boy with the bad pimple who had lost his wristwatch, to pick it up. As the boy bent over, another man goosed him hard. The men's laughter was hollow and ugly.

Back in the barracks, wrapped in a blanket, Brubaker looked for a place to spend his first night. Passing that sitting area in the rear of the barracks where Big Wendel's refrigerator stood, Brubaker locked eyes briefly with an old black man, Abraham Cooke, who sat on one of those three privileged beds. The old man had spent his day in the corridor where Brubaker had seen him mopping the floor. No longer out in the fields, no longer entirely a rankman but not a trusty either, this man was an old timer, Brubaker guessed, who had somehow transcended the coercions of the farm. As he passed by, Brubaker spotted what seemed to be a spare mattress rolled up on the floor.

"Sure, go ahead an' take it," Abraham Cooke told him. "Man who had that ain't got no use for it now."

His meaning was clear, so Brubaker scooped it up and went off searching for a place to sleep.

He decided on a bunk which lay directly under a trickle of water falling from the ceiling. Smoothing out his newly found mattress atop the bare springs, Brubaker climbed up and covered himself with his blanket, careful to draw his feet up and away from the falling water. Shifting his position, he settled back to study the room.

A tough kid with wraparound sunglasses and tattoos on his arms sat nearby plunking away on an imaginary guitar and singing. This was Larry Lee Bullen.

His song was punctuated by the sparks and sputters of a naked electrical cord which hissed and flickered overhead.

Brubaker, listening to these sounds and others, scanned the room. A man hid a homemade knife in his mattress. Faces bombarded him. A cold, heavy, world-weary stare in each one.

Not far off two rankmen moved to each side of a young kid's bunk. He was young and pretty. When the two rankmen pounced on him, he didn't have a chance. The struggle was sudden but predictable, and finally the rankman on his feet covered his buddy and the young kid with a blanket to afford them some privacy in the assault. Nobody intervened. Everyone continued playing cards, writing letters and listening to radios. Big Wendel, the tender, finally moved up and took note of the struggle, but didn't do anything either.

Brubaker felt his fingers tighten on the edge of the bunk as he watched. He would see men masturbate openly while sitting on their beds in here; he would see rough sexual play and actual assaults like this again, but fewer, somehow, than might be expected —perhaps because women were occasionally available to the inmate population and the hope and expectation of a man finding his way into the arms of a female prisoner was always there.

Larry Lee Bullen continued his song without pause.

Brubaker turned away from the assault. He thought of what he had seen in the trusty lounge: the easy living, the trusties strolling from room to room socializing, using their own rooms, lounges and the prison offices as they pleased. They drank beer, played cards and listened to music or watched television.

Later Brubaker would see the full extent of trusty life: coffee and soft drink machines, pool tables, colored TV sets and supply rooms crammed with junk food, beer, new clothes and underwear still in their store wrappings, drugs and hard liquor. The ruling trusties, he would learn, included Eddie Caldwell, who had loaded the wounded escapee onto the bus; Dickie Coombes, the big black who had met them at the main building; the black Fenway Park; Floyd Birdwell; and the affable but dangerous head trusty, Huey Rauch.

It was Huey's voice drifting across the corridor as he spoke to a rankman who worked as a shoeshine boy.

"I be goin' to my house now. Where's my boots?"

The shoeshine boy jumped up, producing a fine pair of boots which had been spit-polished.

Huey Rauch, potbellied and looking drunk, carried a sack of junk food from which he constantly fed himself. He snapped open a package of potato chips as he called for Eddie Caldwell.

"C'mon, Eddie, them new boys who come in today need to go to school tonight. You get up and show 'em what's what."

"Soon as this TV show is finished," came Eddie's reply.

"C'mon, get goin'," Huey Rauch persisted.

A fight broke out in the lavatory, but quickly ended. Big Wendel, the tender, paid it no attention. Instead, he seemed to be looking for someone else in the crowded room.

Another prisoner's tiny radio went on the blink, so

the man began beating it against the wooden headboard of his bed.

Brubaker watched a huge, broad-shouldered Chinese pass by. This was Leonard Ning. He looked like a Tong murderer.

Then Eddie Caldwell and another trusty were standing out in the corridor with the strap.

At this point, Big Wendel found Duane Spivey, a thin kid who sat exhausted on his bunk writing a letter. The wall behind Spivey's trunk was dotted with snapshots.

"Hey, Spivey, they want you at the bars, boy," Big Wendel told him.

"What for?" Spivey asked, looking up.

Beyond, Brubaker noticed that old Abraham Cooke, back there in the area by the refrigerator, had covered up his head with his blanket, rolled over and turned his back on the barracks.

"C'mon, Spivey, c'mere, boy, we ain't got all night," Eddie Caldwell yelled from the corridor.

By the time Duane Spivey had made his way between beds as he shuffled toward the bars, there was fear in his voice. He seemed to know the strap awaited him, although now the other trusty coyly held it behind his back.

"I didn't do nothin'," Spivey argued.

"Yes, you did," Eddie Caldwell answered him.

When Eddie Caldwell unlocked the elephant bars, everyone turned briefly to assess the scene. Brubaker and the newcomers continued to watch after this, but the barracks veterans went on with their business. Then the metal clanged behind Spivey and he was in the hallway. Big Wendel hung a gigantic arm over a horizontal bar and stood there watching.

"I didn't do *nothin'!*" Spivey insisted.

"Take down you pants, boy."

"What about? Tell me what about?"

"Get down, dammit!"

Suddenly angry, the other trusty knocked Spivey down and then started working hard at the belt and pants. Eddie Caldwell took the strap during this struggle.

"I tell you what's about," Caldwell said. "I had me a dream last night, sonny boy, and in my dream you stole my bulldog. Don't you *ever* let me dream you stole my bulldog again!"

"Oh, c'mon, *please,*" Spivey began to yell.

But by this time his pants had been tugged down to his ankles and his flanks were exposed. Caldwell brought the strap down hard: once, twice, three times. This was clearly the night's lesson for those new prisoners in Barracks C.

"How many's that, one or two?" Caldwell yelled at Spivey. "I already forgot!"

"That's *three!*"

Another hard lash followed.

"That's three *what?*" Caldwell yelled.

"That's three, *cap'n!*"

Another lash sprawled Spivey out on the floor. He was lying flat now, so that Caldwell had to turn and lower himself into a new angle in order to strike the blows.

"Oh, that's *four*, cap'n! Oh, cap'n, that's *five*! Oh, cap'n, that's *six!*"

Brubaker turned away, unable to watch anymore of it.

At the end of the beating, several trusties ambled out into the corridor to help Eddie Caldwell, Big Wendel and others carry Duane Spivey back inside the barracks. They tied him to the elephant bars, putting him on display. His buttocks were bleeding and one blow had struck him high across the lower back, leaving a giant welt. He no longer counted or said anything at all.

2

IN the cold morning the work crews formed and jumped aboard flatbed wagons—dobey wagons—which were linked like freight train cars and pulled by a tractor. Armed trusties on horseback kept the peace by riding alongside. Other rankmen shouldering hoes and shovels marched in ragged columns to farm jobs nearer the compound.

Near one of the gates and beneath Tower Number One the old rankman and his victim in Barracks C, the pretty boy who had been raped beneath the blanket last night, balanced themselves barefoot on the wobbly tops of pop bottles set in cases. It wasn't an easy task and failure, Big Wendel had explained to them this morning, would get them both the strap.

"You do that shit in my barracks, you get treated this way. Somewheres else you gonna get the strap right off, but you never gonna go without treatment," Big Wendel explained.

Brubaker watched all this from the longline as he marched. In front of him, Zaranska was trying to whistle his tuneless song again.

"Oh, hey, there's Roy Purcell," Zaranska said.

"Who's he?"

"Office trusty. The warden's asshole."

"Shut it up in the longline," Eddie Caldwell yelled, not seeing who was doing all the talking. He rode horseback, glowering at these lowest of low rankmen this morning.

Roy Purcell was hurrying over to the warden's house. There, Mr. Renfro, the warden, was taking

16

breakfast with his wife and their twelve-year-old son on a small glassed-in porch which overlooked the grove of trees where the women's compound sat. They could also see the main buildings in the distance and the wagons and longlines heading out.

On the living room television set there was a weather report, farm news and a report on the major changes which a new governor had begun to make in the state's highway, sanitation and prison systems.

Renfro was a local man. His wife's brother operated a dairy in one of the nearby towns, and he had dealt with prison labor and with the Wakefield system all his life. Everyone in this part of the state understood the furlough system: prisoners went out on assignment to local farmers. Wakefield machinery and farm equipment was loaned or leased at low prices to the big farms. In fact, everything was involved: sides of beef, state automobiles, building supplies, groceries, drugs. But especially human labor. The rankmen of Wakefield served the community for miles around. Unofficially, of course. And, in turn, favors came back to the warden, staff and a few privileged trusties of the farm. It was a way of life in the delta. Renfro was not appointed to reform or change it, but to administer it.

Some of the dobey wagons filled with men would be met out at the highway by trucks or pickups from neighboring farms. Each would carry trusties, armed and ready, as guards. But the expectations were the same: the rankmen would work hard, give a good day's labor and serve the Wakefield system.

Roy Purcell arrived, knocked and presented himself to the warden and his family. He had a way of bowing, scraping, smiling and being helpful which made him obnoxious to all who knew him—even Renfro for whom he did so much.

He presented the warden with a stack of letters to sign.

"You gonna be comin' down to the office, cap'n?" he asked.

Renfro looked briefly at the letters without answering. Then he concentrated his gaze on the yard.
Two rankmen were washing down a truck which belonged to a candy company across the river.

"I wrote up the letters you wanted," Purcell continued. "Maybe you should read them."

A rankman houseboy brought out more scrambled
eggs. Mrs. Renfro raked a few onto her dish.

"You give your brother a call," Renfro told his
wife. "Tell him I ain't sending but ten boys over to
wash out his milking machinery on Tuesday."

"He wants twenty," she said in a whiney drawl.

Purcell gathered the letters, stacked them and edged
them toward Renfro's elbow once more. The report on
the governor's new plan for the state droned on and
on.

"Shut 'at damn thing off, Purcell," the warden finally said by way of acknowledging his clerk's presence.

Fumbling with the remote control, Purcell obeyed
and the room fell into silence except for Mrs. Renfro
eating her scrambled eggs.

In the fields that morning the new rankmen dug up
the stubble of last year's corn with pitchforks and
rakes, then hauled it to fires which burned around the
perimeters of the field. The men shivered with the cold
and lingered near the fires as long as possible. Brubaker and the new men never got near the fires, for
they crawled behind those clearing the stubble and
planted onion sets. They were on their hands and
knees in the cold, damp earth. Brubaker wanted to
work hard just to keep warm, but even that wasn't
possible because those ahead of him dallied at the fires
so long and slowed the process. It was backbreaking
hand labor and he could only raise his eyes and ob-
serve the longline procedure as he waited in those
frigid intervals.

The trusty guards, all mounted, rode among the
workers dressed in warm jackets, smoking cigarettes
and sipping hot coffee. They carried either shotguns

or high-powered rifles. Already they were thinking about their noon meal, and blazing cooking barrels sent up plumes of white steam. Often they gave each other relief, so that the man on the horse would climb down and go stand at the chuck wagon and the cooking barrels, warm his hands and send back the sound of laughter across these frozen rows.

A gunshot rang out and Brubaker looked up to see a trusty lower his rifle and then stroll over among a group of startled rankmen, where he picked up a dead rabbit. He had paid little concern for the men close to his kill.

An old hand next to Zaranska used this momentary diversion to wolf down several small onions instead of planting them.

By eleven o'clock they had been in the field five hours. At that time a dobey wagon arrived with two barrels of swill for the rankmen.

Eddie Caldwell was there too, on horseback, looking fierce.

"Make it up! C'mon, make it up!" he yelled, and he turned his mount away from those cold rows, breaking the men away for lunch.

Brubaker and Zaranska worked as servers, dishing out a mixture of watery beans to the other rankmen as they filed by the dobey wagon. It was more hard work, but they appreciated the warmth of the cooking barrels. The men filed along, exhausted and shivering, and took their plates off in search of dry ground, sitting in clusters as they regarded their food. Some were too tired to eat or could take no more of the long-line swill, and so lay among the stubble, shivering and helpless, waiting for work to start again.

Meanwhile the trusties enjoyed a regular barbeque. Alongside the water wagon they were grilling steaks and frying up the rabbit which one of them had killed. The odor of hot coffee wafted toward the rankmen.

Hungry, tired and teased by the good food nearby, the rankmen were touchy. When Glenn Elwood came off the chow line with his plate full of the watery beans, someone let loose a low, sensual whistle in his direction. He turned angrily to see three possible offenders. Sitting a few paces away were two big blacks, Jerome Boyd and Mr. Clarence, along with Larry Lee Bullen, who was talking to himself and particularly crazy this morning.

Glenn Elwood picked out Jerome Boyd, the strongest and perhaps the most extraordinary physical specimen on the longline. He charged, knocked Boyd over and began to pound wildly with his fists—actually landing a blow or two.

Mr. Clarence, one of the older but stronger rankmen himself, saw this attack in racial terms. He kicked Glenn Elwood square in the face. There was the sound of breaking bone. Then Jerome Boyd turned on Larry Lee Bullen. Picking up a hoe handle while Mr. Clarence kicked Glenn Elwood again, Jerome Boyd knocked Bullen's lunch off his lap. For a moment Bullen remained motionless, staring at his empty lap. Then suddenly he had a weapon pulled from his legging, a shiny potato peeler. Slashing the big black's ankle, Larry Lee Bullen dropped his opponent to the ground in one swift movement. Then Bullen was on him, sticking the potato peeler up his nose.

"I'm not gonna cut you, nigger, I'm gonna kill you," he said, and Jerome Boyd seemed to know that Bullen meant it and went limp.

Brubaker watched all this from the dobey wagon. Glenn Elwood tried to climb Mr. Clarence's leg, but he was too weak. He spat out a front tooth. Then Eddie Caldwell was there.

"Gimme that weapon, boy," he told Bullen.

Larry Lee Bullen handed over his weapon. With the potato peeler out of his nose, Jerome Boyd looked very relieved.

"Thanks for helping me, man," Elwood said to Bullen.

"You the dumbest asshole," Bullen told him in reply. "Ain't you already got enough comin' down on your head?"

The trusties from the water wagon had gathered around to grin at all the excitement. They chewed at their steaks, eating with their fingers, cups of coffee steaming in their hands, as if they were watching a cockfight or a football game.

In another minute Eddie Caldwell had Bullen and Elwood stretched out on the ground, their pants down around their ankles, while another trusty brought the strap.

Brubaker came over so that he could see Bullen's face. He seemed remarkably calm and accepting of his fate.

"On you face in that dirt, Bullen," Caldwell told him.

Brubaker found himself shivering again—from cold perhaps, but his nerves were singing with anger and shame.

"Gotta learn these boys 'bout startin' fights or they gonna end up down in Camp Five," Caldwell announced to everyone.

Larry Lee Bullen took the first blow with his arms extended. The leather cracked on Bullen's backside, but it was Elwood, lying next to him, who let out the scream.

Brubaker could see Bullen's downturned face. He wore a crazy smile which didn't alter as he took the rest of his licks. A trusty sipped at his coffee while leveling his shotgun at Mr. Clarence and Jerome Boyd. They were next and their faces bore no expression at all.

That night when everyone got back to Barracks C, they saw Duane Spivey still hanging on the elephant bars.

3

BRUBAKER stood among those in the mess line, freezing, grabbing his arms for warmth. The line stretched from the mess hall outdoors and across the yard. By the time a man had stood out there beneath the shadow of Tower One and had reached the mess, his teeth rattled and he could hardly hold the bent spoon to eat his morning bowl of mush.

Brubaker reviewed things to keep his mind off the cold. He had learned the brutal system of trusty guards. The trusty system went deeper into prison life than anyone would have guessed; the trusties had the run of the office, Purcell the trusty clerk managed all the paperwork and rules were made and enforced by trusties. There was an active furlough system which put the inmates into servitude—a rough slavery—at neighboring farms. There seemed to be no food, so where was the money, small though it was, which the state had appropriated? No clothes, no bedding, no medical supplies, no decent structures: everything was threadbare and worn. And the result was that prisoners—those unlucky enough to remain rankmen—had to pay for each morsel of real food and each essential service in an intricate system of corruption.

He stood in the middle of the yard, looking out through the maze of wire fences toward the distant fields and levee.

The men themselves took his thoughts too.

Larry Lee Bullen was a simple burglar, but in prison he was the escape artist. He had been off the

farm lots of times. That's why they were quick to beat
him, Brubaker decided, when the fight broke out in
the field. And he would escape again. He had a deep,
almost wonderful craziness in his eyes; deep down, he
was a free man and they couldn't hold him. The craziness said, "There, I'm free, you'll have to kill me to
hold me," which, of course, they were probably willing to do.

Zaranska was a likeable bastard, the crooked car
salesman type. He had landed in Wakefield this time
for altering the books for a small upstate company. A
little here, a little there, a slight modification in the
books and Zaranska was able to buy a car, those
white plastic shoes which were his no more and a few
nights on the town with his girls.

Glenn Elwood was a tough kid, a car thief. His
character wasn't formed yet—just the hard veneer.
But Wakefield, Brubaker knew, would set him in his
bad ways once and for all.

The big blacks Mr. Clarence and Jerome Boyd had
practiced armed robbery on the outside. Inside, they
were physical brutes, and so hadn't suffered some of
the indignities of smaller men. They believed they
were inside Wakefield because they were black—
which had to be partially so. The majority of the inmate population was black, a tribute to conditions
outside, no matter what the government sociologists
could say about it.

Slowly, thinking on all this, Brubaker made his way
inside the mess hall. His bones seemed brittle and the
warmth failed to help.

Two hundred rankmen were eating in silence this
morning. All of them were exhausted and cold already.

Inside the guard cage a trusty was eating a thick
bacon and egg sandwich. His shotgun lay on his lap.

Brubaker did not yet know the trusties. But he
would. As he passed the steam tables, he tried to
piece together all he had heard about Eddie Caldwell, Huey Rauch, Dickie Coombes, Floyd Birdwell,

Roy Purcell and the others. His hands were still trembling with cold as he raised the tin cup of weak coffee
to his lips and moved on.

Sitting in silence at his awful meal, he made a
quick list. Eddie Caldwell's pleasure was being the
head tough man. Wakefield was his sadistic club, a
place where he could bully others, chase escapees,
carry his firearms, sit proud on his horse. Huey
Rauch, as best as Brubaker could tell, was the ram-
rod of the furlough system; he saw to it that men
were parceled out as cheap labor. He was also deeply
involved—Brubaker didn't know how—in the finan-
cial manipulations of the prison. Floyd Birdwell and
other trusties, they all had a hand in the deals. The
trusties always had beef, for instance, but where did
it come from? And liquor and hardware. And the
women prisoners. Talk was that the trusties used the
women, and Brubaker didn't doubt that a female
body at Wakefield was just another piece of barter.
Dickie Coombes had a special relationship with the
black inmates; he kept them in line and made enough
deals to keep Wakefield from erupting in racial wars
Purcell was slimy; the office clerk probably knew
more than anyone else.

Brubaker finished eating and went toward the infirmary. There the men gave blood for cash.

He hurried across the yard again. His body was
just beginning to warm. Wakefield, he thought, hurrying along, boggles the mind. Its tradition was corruption. And its complexities were almost more than a
single individual could get his thoughts around.

A half-dozen rankmen were giving blood, being serviced by a trusty orderly who kept shoving a
less-than-sanitary set of needles into their arms. A
sign on the wall read: 4 DOLLARS A PINT TODAY.

Zaranska dug a wad of cotton out of a box and
stopped up the hole in his arm where the needle
had just been pulled out. The trusty orderly counted
out three singles from his own wallet.

"Hey, sign says *four* today," Zaranska complained.

"Don't believe what you read," the orderly told him.

Brubaker, watching this, was present when Dr. Fenster, a free-world physician dressed in a suit and tie, came rushing in. As Zaranska pocketed his money and left, the doctor wanted to attend to his duties quickly and be gone.

"My hospital call me?" Dr. Fenster asked the orderly.

"Yessir, twice."

Clearly, Brubaker understood, the doctor gave no more attention to his hospital on the outside than to his Wakefield patients.

In the next room, wrapped in filthy dressings, was the wounded man from the bus. Still alive, at least, Brubaker could see.

"Next," the orderly called, and Brubaker stepped forward with his sleeve rolled up.

With money in his shoe, Brubaker worked another day in the fields. He didn't know if he could make it because of hunger. Even after the noon meal his insides rumbled and weakness overtook him. He was forty years old, in shape, but this was back-breaking labor without nourishment.

Then, after another almost sleepless night in the barracks, Dickie Coombes assigned him to compound duties.

By noon he had worked his way around to the rear door of the kitchen where he could see the trusties eating inside the kitchen area, sitting at tables with steaks, bacon, eggs, potatoes, salads and toast on their plates.

A rank server poured slop into a barrel at the back door.

"What do I do for some real food?" Brubaker asked him.

"Same as like in a restaurant," the man told him.

Brubaker studied the kitchen waste in the barrel before the rank server clanged the lid on it. He could have eaten that. His hunger was all-powerful now.

Inside the kitchen Eddie Caldwell shoved back his plate with a half-eaten steak on it. He smoked a cigarette and flicked ashes onto the plate beside the piece of meat. The rank server came back from the rear door and asked, "You finished with that, cap'n?"

" 'At's worth a buck to me," Caldwell said, pointing to the piece of meat with his cigarette.

The rank server forked the steak and carried it to the back door for Brubaker. By this time, though, Larry Lee Bullen, a rake in his hands, had come looking for food, too.

"Last one. A dollar fifty," the rank server told them.

"Okay, I'll take it," Brubaker said.

"Two," Bullen added.

Brubaker turned and locked eyes with Larry Lee Bullen.

"Two fifty," Brubaker said.

"Three," Bullen quickly added again.

Brubaker shook his head. It was too much. In spite of his payment for a pint of blood, he had to keep money in reserve.

"Sold," the rank server said in the momentary silence.

While the rank server went back inside the kitchen to give Eddie Caldwell his share, Bullen cleaned the ashes off his steak and began to eat it. Brubaker watched in silence.

"You just cost me an extra dollar," Bullen said with menace.

Brubaker could only walk away.

That same hour he sat in the mess hall eating a thin mush with a few beans. He spotted a worm wriggling on the end of his spoon. Holding it up, Brubaker studied it for a moment.

"Hell, eat her. She's protein," a nearby rankman told him, and the remark got an amount of laughter.

Brubaker dropped his spoon in his plate and stared at the wall beyond the steam tables.

The next day Brubaker was at a privately owned

lumberyard with a Wakefield crew of twenty men. They worked with cant hooks to roll enormous logs into an area where a forklift grabbed the timber and set it up on a debarking machine. Above them was a sign which read: WOODWARD LUMBER/OUR WOOD'S AS GOOD AS OUR WORD: C.P. WOODWARD.

The men worked steadily under civilian supervision and the watchful eyes of trusty guards. Rough-sawed planks stacked up beside a loading dock where trucks came and went.

Brubaker had his first good look at Huey Rauch, who was meaner in his way than Eddie Caldwell. Rauch strolled around among the rankmen sipping at a bottle of beer. That afternoon he began selecting men from the work crew for another assignment.

"Zaranska, Ning, you, get over here," he called out.

A closed-bed Wakefield truck arrived, a signal to Larry Lee Bullen that a soft job might be coming up.

"Lemme go with 'em," Bullen said to Rauch.

"You—in the truck," Huey Rauch called out, deliberately passing over Bullen.

At this point the lumberyard owner, C.P. Woodward himself, crossed the yard toward Rauch. He was obviously in a hurry and unhappy.

"Now, Rauch, where you takin' those boys? I gotta get this stuff milled and stacked *today*! I gotta tell my insurance company by Friday what I got on hand!"

"Sorry, my count's down, Mr. Woodward," Rauch answered. "I got ten boys over at the U.S. Marshal's house trimmin' his trees an' another dozen over at Mr. Mawger's car lot waxing up a new shipment of waggons."

"Don't tell me about other people's problems."

"Here, got somethin' for you," Rauch said, reaching into the truck seat producing a big package wrapped in white butcher's paper.

"I don't need no gift. What I need is labor."

"This is sirloin tip for you, Mr. Woodward, but I gotta run a quick errand with these boys."

"Warden Renfro's gonna hear direct that you let me down."

"Ain't gonna let you down," Rauch assured him.

Huey Rauch clearly enjoyed wheeling and dealing in the outside world. He was a man with power —slave labor from Wakefield. It amused him, Brubaker decided, to handle a businessman like Woodward.

By this time Brubaker, Zaranska and Ning were in the back of the closed truck as Rauch slammed the door on them and bolted it. They were taking a ride with a side of beef which hung from a hook and swayed as the truck lurched into gear.

"Lordy, wish I had myself a barbeque fire," Zaranska said wistfully.

Ning, saying nothing, produced a thin, razor sharp knife and cut himself a slice of the beef. Brubaker's eyes widened.

"Sir, would you mind loanin' me that blade for a minute?" he asked, and Ning, in response, gave him both the knife and a thin smile.

Before reaching their destination, the rankmen had themselves a meal. It was mostly dark in the back of the closed truck, cold and difficult to stand, but they enjoyed themselves.

In a few minutes they arrived at Pinky's Cafe Bar. Rauch, still nursing his beer, went inside. It was afternoon, not a customer anywhere, so Rauch went around behind the bar and began filling his beer bottle at the tap.

"I'll do that for you. Don't go fucking with my bar," Pinky said, coming out of the back of his place. He was a corpulent man with thick sausage fingers. "You just get me my meat."

By this time, Brubaker and Zaranska were carrying the side of beef into the cafe under the guard and supervision of the trusty driver. Ning moved ahead of them, pushing chairs aside so they could carry their load into the kitchen.

"Right into the freezer," Pinky ordered them. "And what the hell is this? You tol' me two steers. That ain't no two steers."

"Pinky, I just couldn't this week," Rauch tried to explain.

Pinky finished drawing Rauch a beer, then opened his cash box. He began counting out payment in ten dollar bills.

"Don't tell me couldn't," Pinky went on. "Suppose I can't spare you no beer this week? Then what?"

As the men argued, Brubaker noticed a girl who had appeared at the rear of the kitchen. For a moment, she looked as if she might speak to him, then Brubaker saw her catch sight of Huey Rauch. As Rauch continued talking with Pinky, he motioned for the girl to leave again. Brubaker, getting the beef into the freezer with Zaranska, watched the whole thing. Quietly, the girl slipped back through a rear doorway—out of Pinky's sight—and waited.

"Where's Carol at?" Rauch was asking Pinky.

"Back at the house, I reckon."

Moments later as Brubaker and Zaranska hung the side of beef in Pinky's locker, Rauch slipped back to the rear door in the kitchen where the girl waited for him.

"Carol, honey, you comin' to see me tonight," he said to her.

"Can't come out there tonight," she answered. "My brother's got me workin' here until after midnight."

"Oh, no he don't," Rauch told her. "I just bought you the night off."

On the way out of the kitchen, Zaranska swiped a can of peas from a table. Again, Brubaker, Ning and Zaranska had a brief meal during the ride back to the lumberyard. Opening the can with Ning's dagger, they sat on the floor of the truck, rocked back and forth, and ate English peas with their fingers. Zaranska and Ning talked about Pinky's sister, Carol, and about

Huey Rauch's good luck, but Brubaker again was figuring all the many connections and deals of Wakefield Farm.

Back at the lumberyard, work had piled up in Rauch's absence. As the rear of the truck was opened and Brubaker and the others piled out, rankmen worked with the forklift stacking lumber. Larry Lee Bullen worked a conveyor belt while trying to pull a large, painful splinter out of his hand, but Floyd Birdwell shouted at him and rushed him.

"Damn!" he yelled. "Your comfort don't mean nothin' to me! Git goin'."

"I can't keep up when I'm hurtin'," Bullen complained. "I gotta stop a minute!"

Huey Rauch arrived in a fury with Birdwell, the other trusties and all the rankmen.

"What the hell you guys been doin'?" he shouted. "This shit's supposed to be piled up already!"

C.P. Woodward appeared at the door to the mill, glaring down into the yard at Rauch, Birdwell and the others.

"We gonna keep 'em workin' all night!" Rauch yelled at Birdwell. "It don't make me no difference! We gotta do this for Mr. Woodward!"

Larry Lee Bullen, exhausted and angry, heard this threat and it was too much for him. As a truck pulled away from the nearby loading dock, he managed to snap a chain lock which held its stack. Several tons of lumber slid into the yard, scattering a pile of logs, causing trusties and rankmen to dive for safety. A barrel of kerosene was knocked over. A dog yelped and fled. The truck stopped with a squeal of brakes.

Huey Rauch, his fists in the air, stormed around in a circle. Mr. Woodward and his civilian workers ran everywhere, pointing and shouting.

"Where's the sonovabitch rankman 'at did this?" Rauch yelled.

Jerome Boyd, flicked his head toward Bullen, who

by this time stood at his conveyor belt once more looking innocently interested in all the ruckus.

Huey Rauch came face to face with Bullen. They stared at each other for a long moment, then Rauch backhanded the rankman and knocked his wraparound sunglasses off. But Bullen didn't flinch. As Brubaker and the others looked on, a heavy silence gathered in the yard. Bullen was more defiant than Rauch or anyone else understood; his crooked smile revealed it, and the deep craziness that was there. Huey Rauch suddenly knew that he could do no more.

That night in Barracks C the rankmen sagged in their bunks as usual, while Big Wendel shuffled around selling sandwiches out of a basket.

"Last chance to be smart and buy peanut butter 'n jelly for sixty cents," Big Wendel carried on. "Okay, okay, you assholes, it just went up to seventy-five! Now there's vitamin B-1 in peanuts case you too dumb to know that!"

Brubaker had managed to stand near the old black man, Abraham Cooke, who sat on a stool beside Big Wendel's refrigerator. He wanted to speak with the old man, but didn't know how to begin because Abraham Cooke clearly didn't want to speak to anybody.

At that moment Eddie Caldwell and Floyd Birdwell appeared in the corridor and rattled the bars of Barracks C.

"Larry Lee Bullen! Up at the bars! C'mere!" Caldwell yelled out.

Inside, men wandered around with sandwiches. A few came straggling out of the lavatory, but no one except Bullen, who raised his head and eyes from his bunk, paid attention to the summons. It was somebody else's worry. Brubaker, though, stepped forward to watch.

"Come on, Bullen, don't waste nobody's time," Big Wendel called.

Larry Lee Bullen, knowing it would be worse if

he didn't, rose from his bunk and obeyed. Eddie
Caldwell unlocked the door to the barracks.

"C'mon, you got a phone call," he said, as they
escorted Bullen into the corridor. As the words were
spoken, they had to grab Bullen's arms. Two other
trusties came up to help. Bullen was screaming and
kicking now, but four men had him. They pulled him
along the corridor to the stairway at the far end.

"What's that mean?" Brubaker asked Abraham
Cooke. "What's a phone call mean?" The old man
drew away.

"They reverse the charges," a nearby rankman said.
It was a hard and cryptic explanation.

4

In the early morning shadow of Tower Number One, Dickie Coombes was choosing work assignments for the blacks and Huey Rauch was choosing for the whites. When they got to Leonard Ning, the only Oriental anyone could ever recall being at Wakefield, they fell into a momentary dispute.

"He ain't no white," Rauch argued.

"Not one of us either," Coombes asserted.

"Then I say put him on the shit detail."

"Good enough."

"You too, Collins," Rauch said, pointing to Brubaker. "And Bullen. You, too. Shit detail. Seeing's how you got refried shit for brains anyhow this mornin'."

In truth, Bullen looked awful, so that Brubaker took his arm and helped lead him toward the latrine wagon. Bullen's strength was gone too, so that he leaned against Brubaker heavily.

They waited at the latrine wagon while Floyd Birdwell stopped it at the kitchen door and went inside for an extra cup of coffee. The sun was not yet high enough in the sky for Birdwell, so Brubaker spent the time talking to Bullen, trying to get Larry Lee to come around.

"What'd they do to you?"

Bullen just mumbled.

"You going to make it?"

Bullen worked his mouth, but words wouldn't come. His head lolled to one side. Brubaker tried to get him talking about his many escapes, but Larry Lee seemed hurt and vague.

Larry Lee Bullen was one of Wakefield's escape artists and Brubaker had already heard all the stories about him in the barracks. He had once floated down the river on a huge log to the point at which it joined the Mississippi. He had meant to float all the way to New Orleans on that magnificent spring torrent, as the story was told, then join the crowd at the Mardi Gras, get laid and get lost. But they caught him downstream, three bridges away. Twice he had been caught on the grounds at the farm. The dog boys had beaten him up, the trusties had whipped him with the strap, the warden had given him a few licks and then he had been thrown into solitary confinement. But once he made it to St. Louis and lived there for a year. After being gone so long, he wasn't really punished for that escape. The trusties and his fellow rankmen seemed proud of him for it; he had made it out of the state, had lived with his wife and only a check of his social security number when he tried to get a job had sent him back.

Bullen's eyes were glazed now, but Brubaker continued to try to get him talking.

"The telephone," Brubaker began again. "That's one of those old fashioned ones with a crank, isn't it?"

Bullen's eyes opened and closed.

"Do they put wires on you?" Brubaker went on.

Bullen tried to focus his gaze and almost smiled in the attempt.

"They put wires on your body where it doesn't show, then they run the electrical current through you, right?" Brubaker asked him.

Bullen worked his lips into words and managed to ask, "Hey, listen, what're you in here for?"

"I was in politics, but asked too many questions," Brubaker said vaguely, smiling.

A half hour later they were at Wakefield's death row with Floyd Birdwell, Leonard Ning and the death row trusties with shotguns. Bullen, ashen and still nervous and tired from his ordeal the night before, shuffled in and out of the cells carrying slop buckets.

Death Row was a tight quadrant composed of a dozen cells which faced toward each other and a small central courtyard. There was no daylight except in that courtyard, so that twelve men idled in a dark solitary confinement. While Bullen staggered around cleaning their toilets, they doubled up two to a cell. Procedure was simple: Floyd Birdwell went in with the keys and a shotgun, unlocked a cell, stood back with the gun leveled and allowed some unfortunate rankman to come within arm's length of those condemned men. After cleaning each cell, Bullen's duty was to bring Brubaker and Ning a full bucket and to get an empty one in return.

There were two inches of standing water in many of the cells and the sound of an old sump pump going.

Brubaker, who carried the filled bucket to Ning, who sat atop the latrine wagon, got sick to his stomach. A black trusty kept both Ning and Brubaker covered with a scattergun, but his real attention was on Dickie Coombes, the giant of all the black trusties, who stood in the bright slant of early morning sunlight lifting weights.

"Oh, God," Leonard Ning said, as Brubaker brought another load. He was holding his nose, but getting sick.

Then the commotion started.

Floyd Birdwell, scared as always when on this assignment, had failed to properly relock one of the cells. As Larry Lee Bullen emerged, gagging, from another clean-up, he was grabbed around the neck by Walter Clark, an oversized black maniac—as Floyd always called him—who had eased his door open. With his arm locked around Bullen's neck, Walter began to drag his victim around like a rag doll. His screams were high-pitched and awful. Leonard Ning, sitting up there on the latrine wagon, seemed to change color—for the second or third time during the morning.

"Get the *man* in here!" Walter screamed. "Gonna rip this cat's head *off!* Get him in here!"

Floyd Birdwell, armed only with a mere shotgun, did the wise thing: he fled the cellblock. The other condemned men cowered back in their cells. They had never wanted any part of Walter Clark when he was locked up nearby.

Bullen was choking, his eyes already bulging.

"I got to talk to the man *now!*" Walter Clark screamed. "Where the man? Where he at?"

Dickie Coombes, still exercising over in the recreation area, dropped his weights and came running.

Leonard Ning took the opportunity to get as far from the stinking latrine wagon as he could safely go without being shot as an escapee by a tower guard.

"I hear his neck a-snappin'!" Walter yelled. "Get me the *man!*"

"We hear you, Walter!" Floyd Birdwell called back.

"Give me the man and give me some respect!"

Brubaker turned to the death row trusty, standing there with his shotgun pointed up in the air, and asked, "What's he after? What man?"

"The warden," he was told.

"I'll go get him!" a rankman said, running off.

Walter thumped around the courtyard, terrorizing the other prisoners and choking poor Bullen. Then suddenly he broke into song in a deep bass voice.

Brubaker couldn't wait any longer. Grabbing the cell block keys away from Floyd Birdwell, he started inside.

"Which key's to this door?" he yelled back.

"Big square one! You plannin' on goin' in there, worm?"

"That's right," Brubaker told him.

Bullen kicked and gagged as Walter Clark swung him around.

"Them little keys is for the individual cells," Floyd

Birdwell called to Brubaker. "Got 'em numbered 'n everything! Nice knowin' you."

The siren went off from the tower. Dickie Coombes and a couple of other trusties came running back across the yard.

By this time Brubaker had let himself into the commons and had relocked the barred main door behind him. Walter watched him do this with some consternation, noting that the rankman was unarmed.

"You got five seconds to get me the man!" Walter Clark screamed at the top of his voice. "One! Two!"

"Hey, Walt, whoa, let's talk this over! Huh? What say?" Brubaker said, advancing. His hands were up, gently pushing, as if to hush the man's hysteria.

"Who the fuck are you? Gimme the *man!*" he yelled, then he broke into song again.

Brubaker came another step.

"I *am* the man—the new man," he revealed. "I'm the new warden here. Henry Brubaker."

Floyd Birdwell, looking into the compound from the outside, broke into laughter. But not Walter Clark. The big black man stared Brubaker straight in the eye and dropped Larry Lee Bullen to the floor. Gasping, his victim crawled off into a corner.

"What the hell's going on in there?" Dickie Coombes asked Floyd Birdwell.

"Just a little entertainment."

Brubaker went over and checked Bullen's condition. "What's this man's problem?" Brubaker asked.

"He's crazy," Bullen managed to gasp.

Brubaker turned around to find Walter Clark inches from his face.

"Now don't mess with my head. I don't go for no new warden shit," he snorted at Brubaker.

"It's the truth. It is, Walter."

"Then how come you look like a scum bag?"

"I'm fooling those guys out there," Brubaker said quickly, and his words seemed utterly honest and without guile. As he stood up, he winked at Walter Clark. A secret. Walter shot a glance over Brubaker's shoulders at the trusties who peered inside. Brubaker managed a smile.

"Then you gotta paint this place!" Walter insisted.

Brubaker was staring into the eyes of a lunatic and he knew it. An awful silence grew between them.

"What's your favorite color?"

Walter Clark stared, assessing this man.

"Yellow. And I want a pitcher window in my place."

Brubaker, hands in his pockets, faking a casual attitude, began circling, and managed to get Walter Clark circling backward.

"That yours there? The empty one?"

"Yeah, and I want one of them high-low pinto shag rugs 'n' some liquor 'n' a TV set like them fuckin' trusties got! An' some fresh air 'cause I ain't seen the sun in six months, 'n' if you cain't help me I wanta talk to the governor hisself 'cause he say things is gonna change!"

"They are," Brubaker said quietly.

Circling by the door to Walter Clark's cell, he looked in. The plaster had flaked off the walls and floated in a rancid pool of water. There was a single light bulb, no windows, a filthy commode and a broken-down bed.

"Which wall?" Brubaker asked.

"Which wall what?"

"The picture window," he said, still circling and trying to outflank the big man.

Walter regarded his grim little home. Across the courtyard, Bullen drew himself up, cleared his throat, then became absolutely still as he watched and waited.

"Maybe I want a skylight," Walter Clark mused, looking farther inside.

"Show me where exactly," Brubaker coaxed him. He could feel the sweat running off his face as the condemned man stepped into the doorway of his cell. Then he had to make his move. Charging with his head down, he slammed the big convict inside. Walter tore the toilet off its bolts as his shoulder slid into it. Scrambling, Brubaker slammed the cell door and heard its automatic lock click shut.

As Brubaker went over to Bullen, the condemned man rattled the bars of his cell and let out a long, forlorn cry.

"How's it going?" Brubaker asked Bullen.

"Hurts," Larry Lee admitted.

Soaking wet, they made their way to the main door of the compound where Brubaker opened the lock and then returned the key ring to Floyd Birdwell.

"Get this place dried out and painted up," he told the trusty.

"Sure, what color?" Floyd Birdwell answered, amused.

"Any color Walter Clark wants. And see that Bullen gets some medical attention."

Leaving Floyd Birdwell standing there, Brubaker started striding across the yard. Dickie Coombes had to run to catch up with him.

"What've we got in this place? Lunatics and retards?" Floyd Birdwell called after them.

"Where you think you're goin'?" Coombes asked.

Brubaker sidestepped him and kept walking. "To my office," he said, but Coombes was running, skipping and still trying to get in front of him.

"Mess with me now and you'll regret it tomorrow," Brubaker said to him.

"Either we work this out fast or they ain't gonna be no tomorrow," Coombes said. "I wave my hand and that guard tower gonna blow you out!"

"What do you want? Some ID?"

"It better be quick," Coombes said, as they hurried across the yard.

"Article Nineteen, State Penal Code: no individual shall be housed in a facility wherein there is no free circulation of fresh air, or wherein there is less than one square foot access for natural light per three square yards of living space."

"That don't prove nothin' 'cept you can read," Coombes argued.

"Play it smart," Brubaker told him. "If you don't keep walking with me now, you've made a big mistake."

They were almost at the main building and Dickie Coombes had to think fast. Clearly, there was something in this man's face and voice and style. He didn't walk with the slouch of a rankman anymore.

I better go with this, Dickie Coombes decided. Together they kept on walking, reached the main building and without breaking their stride went inside.

5

BRUBAKER stalked down the hallway inside Wakefield's main building with Dickie Coombes walking alongside. They passed the row of old metal file cabinets and turned into the reception area outside the warden's office, where Roy Purcell, the trusty in charge, as usual sat behind his stacks of papers and his communications center, which consisted of three telephones and the intercom.

"Hey!" Purcell said, jumping up as Brubaker hurried toward the warden's door.

"He in there?"

"Not for you! Who the hell—?"

By the time Purcell could scramble around the desk, Brubaker had flung Renfro's door wide open and had vanished inside.

The captain sat behind his desk clipping his fingernails onto a blotter. Seeing Brubaker charging in, he stood up too, scattering papers and accounting sheets which cluttered his desk top. By the time Brubaker had reached the middle of the room, Renfro had his .38 Special out of its holster and had it aimed, leveled with both hands, arms extended, at the intruder.

"Okay, stop right there!"

Roy Purcell and Dickie Coombes stumbled into the doorway. Brubaker put his hands up. But his words were firm.

"Sorry," he said, "I'm replacing you."

Renfro cocked the pistol, but didn't say anything. For a long, thoughtful moment the men observed an uneasy silence.

41

"Coombes, you wanta give me a hand here?" Renfro enquired in a somewhat shaky voice.

"Call Lillian Grey, the governor's assistant," Brubaker told him. "She's on the prison board, as you know, and you can reach her at—"

Burl Willets, a civilian clerk and purchasing agent who worked with Purcell, stuck his head in the room to see what was going on. Willets was the only other civilian beside the warden and the doctor in the prison.

"Who the hell is this person?" Renfro demanded as he stared at Brubaker. His tone was already weakening.

"He just come bustin' right past me," Purcell offered.

"Tells me he's the new warden," Coombes put in.

"My name is Henry Brubaker," he said, slowly lowering his hands. "I didn't want it this way, but this is the way it is."

"Way what is?" Willets said, edging inside the door for a better look at things.

"You're Willets. Earl."

"Burl."

"Right, Burl, Burl. State employee. Purchasing and accounting. Been here—what? —three years next May."

"Five years in June, no, July."

"Your government service ranking is seven. You're due for an in-grade raise next May."

"Yessir," Willets said, impressed. "That's all true."

"Congratulations, Earl," Brubaker said, taking Willets' hand and shaking it firmly.

"Burl. And thanks a lot."

By the time this exchange ended, Renfro began to know. He slowly lowered the pistol. He saw in Brubaker what Coombes had seen out in the yard, a certainty, a determination and a voice which belonged to no mere rankman. And he knew that his own term of office was finished.

It was some hours later before Brubaker and Renfro found themselves together again at the warden's house. State police cars dotted the lawn beneath the cottonwoods that evening; men carrying boxes of Renfro's personal belongings came and went; troopers stood around as if wondering what to do next. Brubaker, still in his prison clothes, talked on the phone to Lillian Grey, the governor's special assistant, at the state capitol. In the room where he stood the only remaining piece of furniture was a large fish tank —Renfro's son's aquarium—containing a single large goldfish which peered out at Brubaker with about the same wide-eyed surprise as all the trusties and troopers who scurried through the rooms.

"I know, just let me try to handle it, Lillian, okay?" he said into the phone. As he hung up the receiver, a trooper, grinning awkwardly, came from the bedroom carrying a garment bag.

Renfro then passed by with his arms full. The family was out of cardboard boxes, so that stray combs, magazines, ashtrays and pencils were strewn on the floors.

"Look," Brubaker said to him. "I know what it's like getting fired for political reasons. I've been on the short end of that myself."

Renfro didn't answer.

Brubaker could see into the kitchen where Purcell helped Mrs. Renfro pack dishes. The goldfish continued to gawk.

Dumping his armload on another state trooper, Renfro turned and passed by Brubaker again.

"But isn't there a way we can talk?" Brubaker asked him. "I'd like you to give me a rundown on day to day operations."

"No warden runs Wakefield," Renfro said. "Trusties don't run Wakefield. It's a system here. This place done run itself."

An hour later, the night dark as could be out there beneath those barren cottonwoods, the trunks of state patrol cars were slamming shut on the personal effects of Captain Renfro. A Wakefield truck had already hauled away the furniture.

Purcell held the screen door open for Renfro for the last time.

"I'll make sure your mail gets forwarded," he promised the warden in his same earnest tone.

"You know, Mr. Brubaker," Renfro said, going down the porch steps, "smartest thing you ever done was coming in here incogniscent. But you shoulda stayed in the ranks. You want Wakefield, then you got it, but you shoulda never stepped forward."

Renfro got into the patrol car with his wife, who was crying. They were off to live with relatives in a nearby farm community. Their easy life at Wakefield Prison Farm was over.

Brubaker watched the car pull away, its lights flashing, and then he strolled through the litter of the house just vacated. In one room he found some old locked file cabinets and as he paused to speculate on what they might contain, Roy Purcell began to whine at his side.

"We can find the keys for those somewheres if you want," Purcell told his new man.

Brubaker blew a cloud of dust off the papers stacked on top of the files. Purcell, getting the message, began the hopeless task of tidying up the room.

"That Renfro was a human pig," Purcell said with disgust. He picked up a wastebasket in one part of the room, then sat it down in another.

"We'll get a crew to clean this up tomorrow," Brubaker told him, and the trusty gratefully stopped. For a moment the two of them stood looking at the clutter.

"I imagine you sure did learn a lot in them barracks," Purcell said brightly.

"Yes, Purcell, I did."

"By the way, I got your suit and watch. Hung 'em in the back room for you."

Brubaker opened an old desk drawer and pulled out a chain of paper clips, lifting it higher and higher until it reached above his head. The chain just kept coming, no end in sight.

"Mr. Purcell, I want a series of interviews. I want to see the dog boys. Get the infirmary staff into my office tomorrow. Tell Willets to compile all his purchasing orders. I want to see the female trusties at the women's prison and the director of the sewing shop over there. You give me a list of all the furlough gangs we've sent out to farmers and businessmen in the area. I want a list of farm machinery and tools —a complete list. Anything else you can think of?"

"Not at the moment," Purcell said, his mouth open.

"And I want the entire inmate population assembled in the yard after breakfast."

Purcell looked worried. "Wakefield ain't big on records of things," he explained.

"Then you got plenty to do," Brubaker said, dismissing him.

There was also shantytown, the stories about mysterious graves on the farm and much more, Brubaker knew. But these things would mean headlines and political repercussions, so he held himself in and waited.

6

IN the first soft light of morning Brubaker stood on the landing of a rickety outdoor wooden staircase above the inmates of Wakefield. The men below were in uneven rows, shuffling and slumping, as the tower guards looked on. Brubaker wore his own clothes now, with a warm jacket, but he knew that many of the men below were cold, so he meant to make his address to them brief.

"Can everyone hear me?" he said to them.

"Asshole," some rankman answered. There was no way of knowing who it was. Silence gathered as Brubaker looked over the crowd of six hundred men. There was Larry Lee Bullen in the front row, his fancy sunglasses in place, looking as arrogant as ever.

"My name's Henry Brubaker and I'm what the governor promised: a reform warden."

"Big fucking deal," Jerome Boyd said from deep in the crowd. Another moment of silence.

Brubaker extended his hand to Roy Purcell who gave him the rolled-up leather strap. Letting it uncoil above the men's heads, Brubaker cracked it hard.

"This thing is *gone,*" he told the men. "Any trusty here wants to go back to raking rocks for a living, just use this leather on any man in your charge."

"What happens," Huey Rauch piped up, "if somebody starts excapin'? You want us to just wave bye-bye?"

"No, shoot the man," Brubaker said flatly. "But *wound* him if you can because nobody's getting pro-

46

moted to trusty or paroled for killing escaping inmates anymore."

"Can't hear you back here," somebody called out.

Brubaker looked at the men, then actually lowered his voice in response to the taunt.

"As of today, no more fifteen hour shifts," he went on. "We're going to figure out some way to make this place produce like a twentieth century farm. And so I want you to go out in those fields and plant vegetables. Then harvest and *eat* them. Instead of the muck they're feeding us now!"

"What about meantime?" somebody asked.

"In the meantime we start making other changes. No more selling blood to buy decent food. The beef we raise on this farm stays here—and gets eaten by everyone!"

"All right," Zaranska said.

"But let's keep it straight. You're here—most of you —because you belong here. Because you don't have much respect for other people or yourselves. So if you want mine, you have to earn it."

"Why should we believe you?" Larry Lee Bullen said, speaking up. Brubaker stared at him. Here was a man whose life he had saved and he was still on nobody's team except his own.

"You have to believe me," Brubaker told them. "You don't have any other choice."

By this time two state police cars, lights flashing, were on the approach road and some of the prisoners had seen them and had become distracted.

The lead car was crammed with troopers. The second car approaching the guard at the Wakefield gate was driven by Captain Gerald Cleaves, head of police in this district of the state. He didn't look as though he enjoyed being a chauffeur or being at Wakefield this early in the morning. Two civilians sat behind him, John Deach of the governor's prison board and Lillian Grey, the governor's special assistant and also a board member. Deach was fifty, a cigar smoker, and tried to act like an authority. Lillian Grey, who had worked

with the governor toward getting Brubaker into Wakefield, was an attractive, long-legged woman, serious
and with a disarming habit of looking at men directly
and boldly and talking straight.

The troopers shut off their bubble light as they
stopped at the gate. The trusty guard, who seemed to
know almost everyone, bent down and peered into the
car windows.

"Mornin' Mr. Deach," the trusty said with a smile.

"You can pass us through," Deach told him. "This
is Lillian Grey from the governor's office, come to see
the new warden."

The trusty took a long look at Lillian Grey's legs
before Captain Cleaves slipped the car into gear and
started them rolling again.

By the time they reached the main building, the
men had been dismissed and the morning longlines
and dobey wagons were on the move.

Brubaker was in his office nervously trying to fix
himself for presentation. He put on a tie, then took it
off. He quickly combed his hair, then deliberately
ruffled it again. As he arranged the papers on Renfro's
desk, he thought, God, I can handle this madhouse,
but I don't know if I can handle the politics that are
going to come down from the capitol. In those seconds
before the delegation appeared, his career passed before his eyes. He had been an army lieutenant when
he ran a small military prison compound in Maryland.
Then he was hired as an assistant warden in Indiana,
but was fired for insulting a superior officer—which
meant, of course, that he was trying to move too fast
for their system. His actual offense had been the effort
to bring college classes into the prison where everyone
—professors, inmates, staff—except the state prison
board had liked the idea. Eventually he had become a
teacher himself and it was at little Price College that
Lillian Grey had found him teaching penology.

He accepted the job at Wakefield because the governor and Lillian had seemed earnest about wanting
real penal reform. It remained to be seen, of course,

whether or not they just spoke with the rhetoric of election politics.

Brubaker was impatient. Boldness suited him. Action rather than the philosophic poses. In life, people's very existence depended on change and real help. Henry Brubaker dreaded the committee, the trade-off and compromise, reports and studies. Too much of life was Barracks C: a desperate game, rotten and tough, where the rules were against those who were already oppressed by rules.

He straightened himself to face the group outside his office. He heard the voices of Willets, Purcell and Lillian. This had to be done. For a moment, he wondered if he might not rather be out planting onions in the morning cold.

But then Lillian came forward and their eyes met. He started to speak, but she spoke first, saying his name as she came across the room, and she grabbed him and kissed him on the cheek. Her perfume was more than he was prepared for. He stuttered his own hello. And although nothing sexual had ever passed between them, there it was: a brief moment in a crowded office inside Wakefield, introductions waiting to be made, duties to perform, things to do. It shouldn't have happened, but to make sure that it had he fastened his eyes on hers a second time before Cleaves, Deach and the others came forward. And it had happened.

"Good morning everybody," he managed to say.

"I see you got things lookin' normal and 'bout the same as always down here," John Deach said with a big grin.

"No, everything's different already," Brubaker replied, and he could detect Lillian Grey's slight wince when he said it.

A long morning followed. Lillian got on the phone with the reporters of the state, John Deach went around trying to find out what he could about Brubaker from Purcell and the trusties and Captain

Cleaves insisted on administering a loyalty oath to Brubaker in all the confusion.

"How old are you? Thirty-nine?" Lillian asked, holding her hand over the phone.

"Forty," Brubaker answered.

While all this went on, he was trying to rearrange his office and to dispose of all of Renfro's clutter.

". . . to serve the people of this state and of the entire United States," Captain Cleaves went on, trying to encourage Brubaker to hold one palm aloft while taking oath.

"Can't we get on with this?" Brubaker asked.

"What it is, see, is it's illegal running a prison without first taking this oath," Captain Cleaves explained.

Brubaker's attention focused beyond the glass partition which separated his office from Purcell's. John Deach was out there laughing and talking with Huey Rauch, he noticed, as if the two were old friends—or conspirators. He tried to dismiss the slight paranoia which came over him.

"Purcell, would you come in here?" he called.

Meanwhile Lillian invented quotes for the press. "Say something like 'events dictated, time waits for no man,' " she said into the phone.

". . . to *serve*," Captain Cleaves insisted.

". . . to serve the people of this state and of the entire United States faithfully and honestly," Brubaker said in a rush of breath.

Everything moved around him in confusion.

Both Purcell and Deach came in. Willets and Huey Rauch watched everything through the glass partition.

"You got some good men on your side out there," Deach said expansively. He was the sort of man, Brubaker found himself thinking, one easily disbelieves.

"Stress that the governor promised to clean up the prisons if elected and that he delivers on promises," Lillian said into the phone. "A week, yes. Brubaker was in as a rankman for a week. A firsthand look at things, yes."

"Wait a minute, Lillian. No publicity about how I came in," Brubaker said, turning to her.

"Hold it," she said into the phone. "This is good strong stuff," she argued with Brubaker. Their eyes still fixed solidly. There continued to be that little electric jolt.

". . . and be loyal to my superiors," Captain Cleaves droned on.

"Lillian, I know what I'm saying. No publicity," Brubaker told her.

"I quite agree," John Deach said pompously.

"Kill that last part," Lillian Grey said into the phone.

"What the hell are these things?" Brubaker asked Purcell about a stack of yellowed papers on the desk.

"Looks like progress reports," Purcell drawled.

"Set up some shelves out there," Brubaker said. "Organize these things. We've got phone books in here eight years old."

"I'll throw them out right away."

"I don't know how you folks ever pulled this off," Deach said in a voice that rang with the tone of public address. "But I can't be kept in the dark on something like this and Lillian knows that now. I explained that to her. Chairman of the prison board is expected to approve of everything pertaining to—"

"Be loyal to my superiors," Captain Cleaves recited, trying to get Brubaker to continue the oath.

"I just hope you're not one of those people gonna start screaming for free-world guards," Deach said to Brubaker.

"With a good trusty system like this working so well?" Brubaker shot back with a sarcasm Deach didn't quite catch. "I don't know yet. How long you been running the prison board?"

"Did I say that?" Lillian said into the phone. "Good, it's brilliant. Print it. Credit the governor."

"Been headin' the board seventeen years this summer," Deach told Brubaker. "And the trusty system does work okay. It saves the taxpayers of this state lots of money. Works good."

At this point Lillian Grey finally hung up the phone. She turned to John Deach and asked, "Well, John, what do you think of our new warden?"

"I'm trying to get a fix on what his first order of business here's going to be," Deach said frankly. He was worried that the trusty system, with all its corruption and interplay with the state's agriculture and business communities, was going to be abolished. Brubaker almost admired the man's sudden frankness in the matter. Clearly the chairman of the prison board had to be tied to all of it.

"Our best bet is to blow the place up and start again from scratch," Brubaker said. His sincerity rocked Deach. Lillian, in spite of herself, smiled.

"You're makin' a joke, of course?" Deach managed to say.

"Of course," Brubaker answered, and the reply didn't ease Deach's apprehensions much.

Within the next hour Brubaker escorted his guests back out to their cars. He strapped on his holstered .38 Special for the occasion, and Captain Cleaves seemed to regard him with new respect. Deach waved goodbye to the trusties who were present and stepped into the car, leaving Lillian and Brubaker together for a few private words.

A longline of rankmen passed. Their footfalls echoed off the brick of the main building.

"Learn much?" Lillian asked him, talking fast and low. Her effusive and take-charge manner was gone. For this brief instant she and Brubaker were friends and conspirators once more.

"Not enough. I've never seen anything like this place."

"That's because there *isn't* anything like Wakefield. But they won't give you money to hire real guards at this time. That's a sore point. You see Deach's reaction. Let's go slow on that one matter."

"I don't need money to start treating people like human beings," Brubaker assured her.

"Just as long as you understand that the problem isn't just inside this prison," she warned him.

"I've still got to do my work."

"But carefully. Slowly."

"I'll try," he promised, and his voice betrayed his impatience.

"This is very important to us, Henry. I'm juggling lots of things right now."

They felt the trusties and Captain Cleaves watching them.

"I'm juggling, too. So go away and let me work," he told her. They smiled at each other. Lillian caught sight of Deach watching them from inside the closed car window. She gave him a smile, a small reassurance that she and the new warden weren't talking about anything important. Then she turned back to Brubaker. Her lips were moist.

"I just want to tell you, sir, that you are . . ." She paused. "One of the strangest individuals I've ever laid eyes on."

John Deach rolled down the window of the police car. "I've got an eleven o'clock appointment, Lillian. What's the problem?" he asked, trying not to look concerned.

"No problem," Brubaker answered. "Lillian was just telling me how you're one of the most . . . punctual men she's ever had the pleasure of dealing with."

Brubaker held the car door for Lillian and she stepped inside and sat down.

"I'll call you in a few days," she said.

"I know you will."

Cleaves was behind the wheel again. With lights flashing the entourage took off again, so that Brubaker was once more on his own.

The rest of that day the main building was all busy activity. Roy Purcell found himself a snazzy green sport jacket and an administrative assistant, a lanky black who called himself Fenway Park. Burl Willets hovered over his invoices, trying to fathom them. Most of the busy work looked counterproductive to Brubaker, but he was amused by it all and had plenty to do himself. Once he overheard their conversation in the outside office.

"I need to supervise a desk like you," Fenway Park told Purcell. "You's overworked there!"

"I got to answer to General Willets here," Purcell explained. "Ain't that right, Burl?"

"You call me by my proper title or I ain't even answering," Burl Willets said.

In the midst of all the hubbub, old Abraham Cooke tried to get into Brubaker's office, but never made it. The supervisor of the women's compound and two trusties came over with some cookies, baked in the kitchen of the sewing factory, but Brubaker, while accepting them, said he would much rather have a written report on conditions and problems.

"And give me a list of what you want over there," he told the women.

Sarah Doakes, the women's supervisor, was a thick-set Dutch type with quick, dark eyes. "You mean a list or a dream list?" she asked the new warden.

"Make it a dream list, why not?" he answered, and they exchanged grins. He told her that he intended to stop—immediately—the women's frequent overnight visits to the infirmary.

"Shantytown, too?" she asked.

"I don't even know what that is, yet."

"You gonna really like shantytown," one of the trusties put in.

Somehow the lunch hour came and went. Brubaker spent the early afternoon eating the cookies and going over whatever records he could find.

"Purcell, get in here!" he called later on, and Purcell, ever trying to please, jumped up and came running.

"Yessir, liked the way you handled ole John Deach," Purcell told him, laughing somewhat more than necessary. "Lotta people in here gonna be happy. Who exactly was that woman with him?"

"I'm sure Mr. Deach explained all that to you," Brubaker said pointedly. Then, "The day I came in here the trusties put a man on the bus. Gunshot wound. Find out if he's back in the barracks."

"I imagine we shipped him over to county hospital," Purcell said with a hopeful grin.

"Well, find *out*. Then I want you to get me a dozen pairs of sunglasses. Can you do that?"

"Polarized? Tinted? I can get you them kind that's like a mirror in front, so people can't see in."

"Just regular sunglasses."

"Look, captain—"

"And don't call me captain," Brubaker said.

"Yessir, Mr. Brubaker," Purcell said, and he took a deep breath in order to make a speech. "And I understand you prob'ly ready to pick your own warden's clerk around here, but I want to make a case for myself. I know the place and the job better'n anyone else. I been captain's clerk—ah, warden's clerk, I mean, for eight years. What you got here is rural people not too good at paperwork. No sophistication. That's just the way they are."

"What're you in for, Mr. Purcell?"

"Nothin' hardly. Holdin' up a card game."

"I suppose they cheated you."

"Yessir, they did. Anyway, whatever you want—"

"Just the sunglasses for now," Brubaker said, watching Purcell's hick style and hustle with a tinge of admiration.

"Sunglasses, right. They all for you?"

"None for me, Purcell."

"Right!" Purcell said, backing out and getting busy.

It was later that afternoon, the sun high in the sky, that big Walter Clark slowly creaked open his door out at the death row facility. Tentatively he stuck out his head—and peered at the day's strange brightness through sunglasses.

"Come on out," Brubaker told him.

Clark edged out into the courtyard along with the other eleven prisoners. They walked with uncertainty, one footstep at a time as if they were feeling ahead of themselves for quicksand. Nearby Purcell stood watching with Huey Rauch and Dickie Coombes.

As the condemned men emerged from the compound, one of them fell down on his knees and rubbed his fingers across the surface of the dried winter grass. Others crept along in the shade of the building.

"From now on these men get out of their cells once a day, not once every six months," Brubaker instructed everyone.

"Yessir," Huey Rauch replied. As he answered, he looked at Coombes, as if to register his disapproval.

The trusties were armed and uncertain too. But the condemned men strolled around in a gentle aimlessness. Satisfied, Brubaker turned and walked back to his office with Purcell sticking close.

In the early evening Brubaker toured the women's facility. It consisted of one large barracks—cluttered with personal items, but considerably more homelike than the men's quarters—a series of rooms which served as offices and apartments for the meager staff and the big work room filled with sewing machines. There was also a wide yard enclosed by chain link fence. The sewing machines, Brubaker noticed, were old and out of repair, but were situated over by the large windows overlooking the river, so that the women, sitting at their assigned duty, could have the best view of anyone at Wakefield. The food was also better, cooked by the female inmates themselves. They ate, Brubaker noted, as well as the trusties.

"Oh, the trusties take care of the girls," the matron told the new warden. "Never worry on that."

Her meaning was clear.

Out in the yard a young black girl sat weeping at an old picnic table which sat beneath the largest cottonwood tree. Her moans kept filtering inside, so that Brubaker wanted to know what was the matter.

"She got in a fight this afternoon and one of the

other girls cut her face with a cap to a pop bottle," Sarah Doakes explained. "She thinks she gonna be scarred for life, but we can't get her to the infirmary."

"Why not?"

"She don't feel like messin' with the men at the infirmary. Anybody here gets sick, that's the last place they feel like goin'."

Again Brubaker got the picture of the life here. The women were in bondage, their bodies on call.

As he strolled through the barracks with Sarah Doakes and the matron, he got a couple of whistles. There were more than two dozen women. A forlorn, lost group, he felt.

"I want most of these women out of Wakefield as soon as we can arrange it," he told the staff inside their offices. "I'll have their records checked over immediately. Most of them are here for prostitution, and have already served too long as far as I can tell. Meanwhile I want this place locked up tight at night. The infirmary is off limits. I'll get a doctor on call for real illness."

"No visitors during the day?" Sarah Doakes asked. "We get a few trusties delivering food and supplies. You might as well know, they get paid for their services back in the work room closet."

"None of that either. It stops right now."

"And what about shantytown?"

"I'll tend to that soon enough. No woman checks out of this place except on my order."

The matron, a woman of about forty who looked much older, a female trusty herself, said, "Some people gonna worry over this. Some of the girls theyselves."

"Any of you found out to be making profits or sexual arrangements or going along in any way with what's been happening here, I'll find the most excessive punishment for you, understand?" Brubaker said, leveling his gaze at them all.

It was dark when he walked back over to his empty house. For the span of that walk, he felt alone and very tired. Once, passing along a darkened lane, a shiver of fear went through him, and he found himself reaching down to his holster and touching the handle of his .38 for reassurance. Wakefield was a pit, and he had to be alert inside it. For a moment, he felt the matron could have killed him. Hostile words and actions were going to be his lot for a while. Change had that effect.

As he cooked his supper that night, he took the scope off a rifle and used it as a telescope to study the main compound and guard towers. Dickie Coombes, his big black body looking somehow out of place inside the warden's kitchen, seemed uneasy as he stood close by. He didn't know why Brubaker had called him over this evening or what he was supposed to do with himself. Outside, rain began to fall, a gentle sound.

The crosshairs of the scope settled on a guard tower where, as well as Brubaker could tell, the trusty guard was looking back at him through a pair of binoculars.

"Tower Six," Brubaker said to Coombes. "Who am I looking at? He's looking over here at me."

"Up there you got yourself Douglas Mizell."

"Who is Douglas Mizell, Mr. Coombes?"

"Forger. Three times grand theft."

"I want you to give me a rundown on every man who has tower duty."

"I do believe that's Purcell's job, sir."

"I only want murderers up there. One time only impulse killers."

"That be takin' a chance, ain't it?"

"It's habituals can't be trusted. Murderers, most of the time, they get it out of their systems. Like you, right, Mr. Coombes?"

"Ain't nobody else in here like me," Dickie Coombes laughed.

Brubaker set the scope down and looked at Coombes, a solid, strong man who had something in his face—character—which could somehow be trusted.

"Back there at the death row facility, why'd you let me go?"

"You the man. You tell me," Coombes answered.

"I figured you just wanted to cover yourself both ways."

"Well, I don't think of myself as dumb," Coombes admitted.

"You're in for murder, right?"

"Hey, I thought we was gonna talk 'bout ways of changin' things around here."

The timer on Brubaker's oven rang and he crossed the kitchen to take his dinner out. Coombes leaned forward to see what the warden was having for supper. There was a foil tray loaded down with Mrs. Paul's Fish Sticks, Krinkle Fries and a pouch of frozen vegetables.

"Sure you won't eat?" Brubaker asked.

"None of that shit, thanks," Coombes answered.

"All this good acreage, good land, livestock, and everybody's starving except you trusties," Brubaker said, beginning to eat. "You know a lot about nutrition?"

"I know 'bout hungry."

"You don't look hungry. You like being a trusty?"

"It better'n bein' a rankman."

Brubaker dipped a fish stick into a jar of tartar sauce, then popped it into his mouth.

"I imagine you've seen a lot of reform wardens, haven't you?"

"They's all reform wardens."

"Renfro wasn't."

"Where the hell you think all them raggedy clothes them rankmen's wearin' come from? You think we got a special factory makes rag clothes? Renfro got 'em brand new. And the clothes you gonna bring in—"

"How do you know I'll do that sort of thing?"

"You gonna be a reform warden who gives us new clothes, same as ever'body else. And you gonna think you done good," Dickie Coombes went on. "They gonna be the rags the next reform warden gonna throw out."

Brubaker dipped another fish stick. He watched Coombes as he ate. Here was a man, at least, who would speak his mind.

"You don't think things can change?"

"Not so damn much, no."

"Well, I think so," Brubaker said.

"The system don't work right if you change a single thing," Coombes told him. "You find out a man's chargin' for laundry, say, an' so you stop him from makin' a quarter on every shirt he washed. You done stopped corruption? Naw, he gonna get in trouble then, 'cause he cain't pay off somebody else. Maybe the next man he cain't work his deal 'cause the laundry man didn't pay him. Then somebody gets killed for not payin'. It's a big mess, see, an' you don't start with no little part of it."

Brubaker sat there looking at Coombes and listening. The analysis, of course, was clear and true.

At that moment the phone rang. His fingers sticky with tartar sauce, Brubaker asked Coombes to answer.

"Yeah? What're you talkin'?" Dickie shouted into the phone. "Security? Anybody hurt? Okay, okay!"

Hanging up the phone, Coombes turned to Brubaker.

" 'Scuse me, captain, are we done here?"

"What's wrong?" Brubaker asked.

"Rank barracks," Coombes told him. "Roof just caved in."

7

BRUBAKER and Coombes ran across the fields in the gentle rain toward the yard and main building.

The rain, falling softly, had finally weighed down the roof and ceiling of the barracks and had caved it in. It had been inevitable. But as they crossed the yard beneath the guard tower, shouting so that a trusty would open the door ahead of them, and as they ran up the stairs in the flickering light and heard the moaning cries and shouts of men in trouble, they were not prepared for what they saw. No one had yet opened the bars, so that inside the barracks a cold, wet, rain drizzled in through a six-foot hole in the roof. Men lay under debris in pools of water, and dangerous chaos existed.

"Who's done what?" Brubaker yelled at Huey Rauch.

"Nobody's done nothin'!" Rauch shouted back. "Waitin' on you!"

Brubaker stared in through the elephant bars. Trusty guards ran around helplessly. Sheets of wet fiber board, timbers and moldings lay everywhere. A ceiling light swung dangerously close to the gathering pools of water, dropping sparks and threatening a fire as the lights blinked off and on.

Dickie Coombes grabbed the keys off the desk in the corridor.

"Get flashlights!" he yelled. Then he found a switch box and pulled the lever. The place turned dark, but the threat of fire and a much worse disaster was averted.

Next Coombes unlocked the barracks. "You stay here and keep yourself armed!" he yelled to Brubaker.

"No way," Brubaker said, and he followed Coombes inside.

Flashlights lit the scene as Brubaker, Coombes and a few other trusties braved the inside of the darkened barracks. Zaranska dragged an injured Glenn Elwood toward the front door. Groans punctuated the shadows. A heap of soggy rubble had fallen squarely on a bed where a man lay groaning and trying to move an arm from beneath it.

The timber was still creaking overhead.

"I want these men out of here, Coombes," Brubaker shouted. "All of them!"

"They gonna move in with you?"

"Put 'em in another barracks, anywhere. This roof may go again. No, wait, the mess hall: take some mattresses in there."

Coombes and Brubaker, lit for a moment by flashlights, looked at each other. The exchange was silent, but clear: Brubaker wasn't afraid of being here, wasn't going to hang back and would work to help. Dickie Coombes gave him a short smile and a nod.

An hour later they had the injured men inside the infirmary. Brubaker was on the phone dealing with the nearest hospital. Rankmen were being carried in by Larry Lee Bullen and others. Zaranska acted like an experienced intern, walking among the beds, checking patients.

"It's just your scalp," he told Glenn Elwood. "You're just losin' blood, nothin' else."

"Goddammit, I can't afford blood," Elwood told him. "That's what I pay for my food with!"

"Here's another who's gotta go to the hospital," Burl Willets called toward Brubaker.

But Brubaker was busy on the phone and angry.

"What the hell do you mean call the *state* hospital? You're twenty miles closer and we've got an emergency! It's raining, I've got only one good station wagon and I can't put 'em in open trucks!"

Dickie Coombes opened the door for Dr. Fenster, who came in looking bored. He smirked as he opened his black bag.

"They're not *just* convicts!" Brubaker yelled into the phone. "They're injured men! A concussion for sure! Some fractures and maybe some transfusions! An hour? Why? What're you *doing?*"

Blood spurted from a man's arm, so that Zaranska called for the doctor to hurry. Dr. Fenster was already beside another man, preparing a hypodermic.

"Doc, over here," someone else groaned.

"All right, two ambulances! I'm counting on that!" Brubaker said on the phone. "And what's your name? Give it to me. Spell it." He wrote down a name on a piece of paper, then ended his call.

"I said I can't afford no more," Glenn Elwood said again.

Brubaker overheard this and came toward Dr. Fenster, who was at Elwood's side.

"What'd he say?" Brubaker wanted to know.

"He's just scared," Zaranska noted.

"Nothing, he's all right," Dr. Fenster said, and he pushed the needle into Glenn Elwood's arm.

"I ain't all right," Elwood said. "He's a bloodsucker and I just can't afford no more. I gotta have my blood."

"Shut up," Dr. Fenster told him.

"Wait a minute, what's going on here?" Brubaker asked.

"I told you to shut up and keep still," the doctor told Elwood.

"Wait, now, you're charging for medical attention in this infirmary, aren't you? You've been *charging* the inmates for what the state already pays you to do!"

"What're you saying?" the doctor said, trying to ignore this.

"You! I'm saying you *are* a bloodsucker!"

Brubaker caught a glance from Zaranska. He had

guessed right, he knew, when he saw Zaranska's nod.

"Don't get excited," the doctor said, moving to another man. "It's been working this way for years."

Brubaker could stand no more. He took the man by his collar, bounced him off tables, backed him across the room, then dragged him through the door. Dickie Coombes opened the door to let them pass.

On the outside landing in the rain Brubaker turned the doctor's face roughly around. A light mist wet their faces. Brubaker's teeth were clenched tight as he spoke.

"Get off this farm and don't ever show yourself around here again," he told the doctor.

"You're makin' a mistake," the doctor argued, but this infuriated the warden even more. Handling his man, Brubaker walked him down those rain-slickened outside stairs and threw him into the mud. A bolt of lightning momentarily illumined the scene. Brubaker's anger had reached a high pitch as he went back upstairs toward the men who needed him inside the infirmary.

"Zaranska!" he yelled as he came back in.

Everyone, both injured men and those helping, had stopped to stare at him. Some of them were smiling.

"Yessir!" Zaranska answered, startled.

"You had any experience in hospitals?"

"Did a little first aid field work in the war."

"Then this is your hospital," Brubaker said.

"What?"

"You're in charge until we can get ourselves a real doctor. Starting right now."

"Well, tell the truth, sir, I—"

"You know as much about it as anyone else," Brubaker told him. "So come on, man, *work* with me!"

A few days later many men were working with Brubaker, while others held back. There were still showdowns and confrontations left, and one of them arrived in a Cadillac Coupe de Ville one morning, gliding through the main gate to receive only a nod of instant recognition from the trusty guard who had previously stopped two cars of state troopers. C.P. Woodward, the lumberyard owner and a staunch user and supporter of the trusty system at Wakefield, pulled up in front of the main building, got out and began fumbling for something in the trunk of the car before going inside.

Brubaker and Willets were busy that morning checking kitchen items. Willets, carrying a clipboard, followed Brubaker on an inspection of the store rooms, pantries and refrigerators.

"Okay," Brubaker was saying, "we took delivery of three hundred cases of chili con carne last week. Now where is it? We've looked almost everyplace."

"Boys musta gobbled it up," Willets offered weakly.

Eddie Caldwell strolled by with a bald, freshly shaved rankman at about that time. Watching them pass, it registered on Brubaker that the rankmen certainly didn't get the benefits of anything as nourishing as chili.

"There's only fifty trusties who could've eaten chili," he calculated, scribbling a calculation on the clipboard note as Willets dutifully held it. "Let's see, seven thousand, two hundred cans divided by fifty trusties come to —one hundred and forty-four cans! I'm not the best at math, Mr. Willets, so correct me if I'm wrong."

They strolled into the mess hall as Brubaker continued to calculate. Rankmen were painting the dirty walls around them.

"Divided by seven days . . . comes to . . . more than twenty cans of chili con carne per trusty per day. Do you have any idea how many farts that is, Mr. Willets?"

"No sir," Willets answered, adjusting his glasses. He was not one to see humor in a boss's observations.

"Willets, are you alive?"

"No, sir—er, yessir," Willets said, confused.

"Well, let's see, our roof fell in," Brubaker said, as they turned into the main corridor en route back toward the office. "And my people here are starving. And paying for the food they do get with their blood. And so I want you to find out where in hell the food is going! Can you try to do that, Mr. Willets?"

"Yessir," Willets said timidly.

They entered Roy Purcell's office now. By the time Purcell rose to his feet, he was faced with an angry warden.

Brubaker pointed a finger at him and snapped, "I want this posted: only regulation clothes from now on are prison issue pants, shirts and boots."

"Boots? We ain't got no boots," Purcell countered.

"Then order them! And no more shaved heads!"

"Acquisitions is Willets' area."

"Then see Willets gets boots ordered for every man here. And crepe soles for the women! They're walking around on cement floors over there in the sewing room!"

"Yessir," both Willets and Purcell said together.

"Sizes!" Purcell said to Brubaker as the warden turned into his own office. "How m' I ever gonna figure out, say, how many size nines?"

Brubaker, not answering, pulled up short as he came through the door into his inner office. There was C.P. Woodward sitting behind the warden's desk using the telephone. On the desk blotter there was a wrapped gift. The businessman got up, extended his hand and put on his happiest and most aggressive manner.

"Goddamn, look at you! New blood!" he said. "'At's what this place needin', all right, fresh air! You're Brubaker, m'I right?"

"That's right," Brubaker answered.

"Well, you sure don't look like no warden!" C.P. Woodward told him. "But here you go, little present. Chocolate prune cake in here. My missus baked it up for you. You gonna like it."

"I hate prunes. They cloud my mind," Brubaker said, but the businessman didn't flinch. His smile seemed fixed in place.

"Did I say my name?"

"Nope, but I know who you are," Brubaker told him.

"C.P. Woodward. Call me Woody. You sayin' we already met?"

"Look, what can I do for you, Mr. Woodward, because—"

"The roof! I come about your busted roof! Purcell here give me a yell, said you declared a state of emergency or somethin'!"

Beyond the glassed-in partition, Purcell and Willets turned their eyes away from this encounter between Brubaker and Woodward and paid elaborate attention to the clutter atop their desks.

"I thought you just sold lumber," Brubaker said.

"Lordy, I sell it, grow it, mill it, hammer it! Got wood in my blood!"

C.P. Woodward pulled a document out of his pocket. He rattled its bulky fifteen pages onto the desk. Watching this performance, Brubaker took a seat across from the businessman—the guest chair.

"Okay, now, you gimme your John Hancock and we'll fix that roof up real good," C.P. Woodward said with a grin.

"Don't you want to go see the barracks first? Take a look at the damage, so you know what you're contracting for?"

"Whatever's wrong, we'll fix, you can bet on that. Way we always do it around here is sign up an open contract, then get the job done!"

"Thing is, I don't think you've ever gotten the job done," Brubaker told him. "You built it badly, then rebuilt it two years ago—and not such a good job then. I want it rebuilt now like it should have been done the first time."

"Sure you do. And don't worry, I can help you out on costs. I'll bill Wakefield just for materials this time around."

Brubaker sat looking across the desk. His jaw tightened.

"This isn't going to cost Wakefield anything. You guarantee your work, don't you?"

" 'Course I do. But, look, Henry, you gotta get on

top of this shit pile around here. I mean, ever'body wants you happy. This job don't have to be *hard*. It can be a very happy job for you!"

"I'm happy," Brubaker said. "I just want that roof fixed right."

C.P. Woodward got up from behind the desk and then walked over and closed the office door. As he did, Brubaker reclaimed his own desk chair and boldly placed the gift near Woodward.

"Now, look, I'm not in the construction business for my health," C.P. Woodward said.

"Or anybody else's health either," Brubaker interrupted. "Your roof, which is only two years old, caved in on my men."

Woodward took a deep breath, trying to calm himself. His smile had long faded.

"I come over here in the middle of my inventory," he said to Brubaker. "Pain in the ass, but busy as I was, I come rushin' over here. And ain't nobody from Wakefield been comin' over to give me a hand lately."

"And never will again," Brubaker told him. "There will be no more convict labor, which is slave labor, as far as I'm concerned."

"No, it ain't. No, no, you got it all backwards, see, because this is a community. People around here could ostracize the prison, but they don't. We accept it. We cooperate. It's a two-way street too, because you be gettin' a lotta nice things from people in the farm supply business, folks in the clothing business—"

"And the lumber business?"

"Sure, like this cake. Point ain't whether you like prunes, point is, this is a gift from a *friend*."

"It's the thought that counts," Brubaker said with pointed sarcasm.

"Exactly. Only smart to accept things, keep your mouth shut 'n' let things run like they've been doin' for years. A hundred years, before we was born even, you 'n' me. I'm talkin' about tradition. Don't mess with tradition, that's what I'm sayin'."

There was a sudden edge in Woodward's voice, a

threat. Brubaker rested his elbows on his desk and stared across at the businessman.

"Tell you what," he said. "I'm gonna fix the roof myself. And you better go do your inventory."

Silence between the two men.

"Lotta people gonna be disappointed in you, Brubaker," C.P. Woodward said.

Brubaker nudged the wrapped gift closer to C.P. Woodward, who picked it up as he got up to go. Woodward also folded the unsigned contract back into his pocket. Together they walked back outside to Roy Purcell's office.

"Get me any contracts and insurance policies we have on that roof, Purcell. I want everything you've got," the warden said. With that, he turned and went back into his office, leaving Woodward standing there with Purcell and Willets.

"You on his team?" Woodward asked Purcell.

It became an uncomfortable moment for Purcell, who squirmed in his chair. Brubaker could see him through the glass partition.

"He's the coach for now," Purcell managed.

"Then it sure is gonna be a short season," C.P. Woodward said, and he walked out.

8

As the days passed Brubaker inspected Wakefield Prison Farm in its many parts. Craziness everywhere: there was an old peck who fished down beside the levee. He was perhaps eighty years old, alone and no longer bothered to report to the barracks or main buildings, for his number had been lost, it seemed, years ago. Old Billy, they called him, and he ran his trotlines for catfish every day. At one time, Brubaker was told, the old man provided a modest amount of fish for the trusty tables inside the gates, but now he let go whatever fish he didn't himself eat. His cabin was built around the low, heavy branches of an old live oak whose shade reached out into the yellow waters of the river itself. A tree house, with rickety steps climbing up into those swaying limbs, everything decorated with catfish skulls and flattened tin cans, a ramshackle, forlorn clutter in one isolated corner of the Wakefield immensity.

"They beat me," Old Billy told Brubaker, "for having me a woman out here onct."

"Is that so?" Brubaker answered. The old man was small and bent, thin as a mere shadow.

"Didn't have no woman at all," he told Brubaker, not even knowing exactly that this was the new warden, if ever he had met the others.

"But I ain't runnin' no more," the old man said. "I used to run, but, shit, no more. They tol' me I'd get turned into fish bait if ever I tried. Ain't movin'."

As best as Brubaker could make out, life became so good for the trusties inside Wakefield that they didn't need the old man's catfish. They traded with area merchants for all they needed. The farm was like a gigantic exchange post: foodstuffs, hardware, clothes and cash coming and going in what amounted to a hefty market. The old providers had disappeared. The truck farm had been mostly abandoned. Old Billy and his kind were forgotten.

Another day Brubaker stopped to visit the dog boys, who were crazy too, in their way. Like Old Billy, they lived apart, though a truck circulated between the kennels and the main buildings daily.

Lean and hard in the stomachs, they were like Olympic sprinters. Every day they ran with their hounds, starting from the kennels and covering most of Wakefield's acreage; they seemed tireless and obsessed with the run itself. Although their principal job was to catch runaways, running with their dogs— through patches of woodland, over the rough ground, along the levee trails, over toward the highway, back again—was their life and reward.

When escapes took place, the dog boys were good at recovering prisoners. But then they were fierce, Brubaker learned. Their daily free runs interrupted, they were likely to give the offender a bad beating before returning him to the compound. What the dog boys usually did was knock out a man's front teeth, a marking which told its own story inside the barracks and became a kind of badge of honor worn by those who had tried and failed to get away. Occasionally they let the hounds chew on the victim a little, especially if the culprit tried to harm the dogs or attempted to throw them off the scent by sprinkling pepper or some harmful chemical on the trail.

"Ever had a man who killed one of the hounds?" Brubaker asked them.

"Aw, sure," one of them answered, and they all squinted at one another and shuffled themselves crablike until they bumped shoulders, their strange way of communicating their little secrets. Brubaker took this answer to mean that any bastard who would kill one of their hounds was as good as dead himself. He stood there at the kennels, watching them—there were six dog boys, all trusties, but a breed apart—and they were like odd, hick cousins, all their gestures and winkings and squintings looking very much the same. That crab-like sidelong shuffle; they looked like they had been dropped on Wakefield from a race of demented gods.

Their cabin was small, a single-room clapboard beside the chain-link kennels. And they slept in there like dogs themselves, huddled together on a communal pallet over in one corner of the room.

"We like it out here," they explained to Brubaker simply. "And we's all habituals. Might's well stay here as get paroled back to the city where we gonna steal shit and bother folks."

Brubaker had the feeling that their records, like Old Billy's, might be lost in the depths of Purcell's office, too.

In Renfro's days a trusty inside Wakefield could win a parole by catching, dead or alive, an escapee. But the trusty's competition was the dog boys; they knew every culvert, every narrow woodland trail, each spot on the river. Usually they had an escapee before half a day could pass, and often they had appeared at the last minute before a convict jumped into a friend's car and thwarted the most well-planned escapes.

The hounds, who ate far better than any rankman, could swim the river and pull a runaway back to shore. They would bite a man in an open field so long as he tried to keep moving, but would only circle him and hold him otherwise. Unless given instructions by their masters, they were not especially vicious. But, like the dog boys, they were a legend of the farm. On rare occasions when a dog boy showed up at the main building, everyone gave him a wide berth. He would have a hound with him, heeling and ready like an attack dog, and at the back door to the kitchen or in the rankmen's corridor—where no one would ever suggest that the hound should be left outside—he would be treated with respect.

"Them guys is the psychopathic elite," Zaranska explained to Brubaker. Good enough as descriptions go, Brubaker thought, after he had seen the kennels for himself.

There were other isolated stations on farm acreage. Barns, two or three guard towers down by the levee— usually unoccupied—and assorted pig pens, cattle corrals, equipment sheds, silos and grease barrels where the dobey wagons clustered like abandoned antiques.

Shantytown, then. Brubaker saw it only at a distance in those first days of his new job. He was driving from the kennels in the farm station wagon when he topped the levee and glanced westward where the river made its widest bend. And there it was: row on row of lean-to shacks and tarpaper houses, with a couple of rusted trailers sitting among them. He was driving in the opposite direction along the levee, late for jobs in the office, and decided against a visit at that moment, but he knew what he was seeing. It was a trusty haven, a place for Huey Rauch, Floyd Birdwell, Eddie Caldwell and the other more powerful white trusties. Even among the trusties, Brubaker knew, there were levels of authority. Dickie Coombes was a man with influence, but mostly as a black man among other blacks who was expected to keep the rankmen of his race in line. There were those with easy jobs, trusty guards, drivers, or those isolated like the dog boys, but the inner circle was small and shantytown was theirs.

Brubaker well knew what he would find out there in the bend of the river. The best of the prison food, amenities and women—both female inmates and girls from outside. It was mostly Wakefield's brothel, he suspected, visited by the special trusties, local farmers, businessmen like C.P. Woodward and a few privileged others. Linked to the main highway by its dirt road, shantytown was the deepest corruption of the

farm. Some link also existed, Brubaker sensed, between it and Pinky's Cafe Bar in town. But, driving
on and not looking back, Brubaker decided not to
visit shantytown just yet. Better to lull these men for
the time being. Better to let them think that the new
reform warden might let their most treasured place
alone.

That night he ate in the mess hall with all the others
—rankmen and trusties sitting down in the same
place, eating the same food, except at separate tables
in strict segregation.

Walls and tables had been painted now. There
were new cups and trays and the menu consisted of
beef stew, salad greens and cornbread. As Brubaker
came into the hall and went along the steam tables
with his tray, a general silence fell over the room. He
was not popular—in spite of all the changes and im-
provements—and was only slowly learning all the
reasons why.

Carrying his tray, he sat with the trusties: Purcell,
Birdwell and Coombes, who got up to leave the table
when Brubaker appeared.

"What's the matter with him?" Brubaker asked.

"Don't want to eat with you," Floyd Birdwell said
simply.

Birdwell was tall and freckle-faced, and kept a tooth-
pick in his lips even when eating. On the outside he
was a hijacker, having stolen a number of truckloads
from New Orleans to Kansas City.

"There's what we call in the barracks a crawler,"
Birdwell explained as Brubaker began spooning in
the beef stew. "This guy crawls along underneath the
beds late at night after ever'body is asleep. He cuts
throats. Has hisself a grudge against a feller, say, so
just crawls along in the dark an' cuts the throat. Man
don't do nothing but gurgle slightly when his throat's
cut."

"So?" Brubaker asked, still eating.

"Ever' trusty is afraid of getting stuck. You've put
the damn guards an' prisoners together, see, so it don't

mean but one thing to us. One of us gonna get his throat slit. Those boys do it at night in their barracks an' now they gonna do it to us."

"We can't all eat different food," Brubaker told him. "We've got to get close to each other sometime."

Birdwell got up too and started to leave.

"I tell ya," he said, "I get a lump in my throat in here and *cain't* eat. You got Dickie Coombes mad at you because he done had a nigger try to stick him today. An' you got me with indigestion."

"Sorry," Brubaker said, and he watched Birdwell go.

For a while Brubaker and Roy Purcell ate together in silence. Then Brubaker asked, "Where's Huey Rauch and Eddie Caldwell?"

"Don't ask me," Purcell said, but there was something unconvincing in his voice which said, yes, I know, they're at shantytown.

After finishing his stew, Brubaker got up and left too. On the way out, he instructed Burl Willets to send Larry Lee Bullen over to the warden's house by eight o'clock that evening.

He stopped by his office on the way home that night. On his desk was a list of things to do: collect all weapons, review all women's files, go over invoices. The days seemed short, as if time hurried him along, but he wanted all the big changes—let the enemies come, let Dickie Coombes get mad—before the planting of spring crops.

He decided to hide the list before Purcell or Willets spotted it. If the inmates got news of a weapons round-up, they would be more ingenious hiding their knives and brass knuckles.

He took the station wagon on that short drive over to the warden's house. A dark night. Once he touched the .38 in his holster just to make sure.

The house was still strewn with remnants of Renfro's life there. The dusty file cabinets had been unlocked, adding to the mess, and Brubaker had found enough interesting material that he hadn't ordered things cleaned up because he feared that evidence might accidentally be thrown away.

That night he called Lillian Grey about some of it.

"They write it all down," he told her on the phone. "Their practice has been so damned bold, you couldn't believe some of the items I've found. They've had guys from this prison building swimming pools for people. Prison lumber and prison labor put up a motel for some character over by the interstate."

He nodded and listened as Lillian warned him that he had to go slowly.

"I *am* going slow! Try to believe that!"

A noise across the room caught Brubaker's attention as he talked on the phone. A rat. He saw it edge into view, fearlessly invading the dining room where the phone cord dangled over some of those yellowed documents.

Slowly, as he talked, Brubaker unfastened the holster on his pistol.

"I got a man in this prison doing twenty years for stealing a pig," he told Lillian. "While my kitchen rider, a trusty, loads our food into state police cars!"

More slowly, Brubaker slipped his pistol out.

"I don't know," he told Lillian. "Sure, it probably involves the state police. *Some* policeman or civilian or *somebody* gets most of the beef, ham and chicken that's delivered to Wakefield. And, yes, we're probably going to be stepping on more toes than we imagined!"

The rat nibbled at something in a far corner. Brubaker, listening to Lillian, stood up and stretched the telephone cord toward his quarry. With care, he cocked the hammer on his pistol.

"That's right," he told Lillian. "I'm just warning you because you're going to start hearing things against me. I sent back three cases of Jack Daniels from somebody who called himself William 'Mr. Soybean' Hartnell. For years, it seems, he's been getting most of the bean crop from Wakefield at cut-rate prices."

The rat scurried to another corner. Brubaker, listening to Lillian, picked up the phone and followed it.

"You just stay close to the governor," Brubaker went on. "Tell him about me and C.P. Woodward. And all the rest. Run interference for me just as you said you would, that's all I ask. And, listen, Lillian, can I call you back?"

Brubaker said his goodbye and hung up the phone. The rat stood on its hind legs in another corner as Brubaker, down on his hands and knees, began stalking it.

Suddenly, just as he aimed the .38, his doorbell rang.

"Hold on, just a second," Brubaker called.

A loud knocking started.

"I said hold on, just a second!"

Larry Lee Bullen's head came through the front door. He wore his dark wraparound sun-glasses.

"You say come in?" he asked, surprised to see the warden in this posture, his pistol drawn.

Brubaker didn't know what to say either. Embarrassed, he pointed into the corner. "Rats," he explained. "What can I do for you?"

"I come over to see what you wanted with me," Bullen said.

"Well, come on in." Brubaker was still on his hands and knees. Slowly, giving the rat a last look, he stood up.

"I don' like bein' here," Bullen admitted. "Looks like I'm suckin' up to the man."

Brubaker, shaking his head, motioned for Bullen to follow him into the kitchen. There he offered the rankman a cup of coffee.

"Thanks, no, makes me nervous," Bullen said, declining. His hand was still shaking, Brubaker noticed, from the ordeal with the Wakefield telephone.

"Tell me about that phone call you got," Brubaker asked, taking his first sip and trying to get Bullen to relax.

"Wrong number." Clearly, Larry Lee Bullen wasn't

talking. He pulled a cigarette out of his shirt pocket, straightened it with his fingers and lit it.

"I hear it doesn't leave any scars," Brubaker said. "That so?"

Silence. Brubaker watched Bullen over the rim of his coffee cup.

"Well, I see your hand still shakes," he said. "So I'm transferring you to the infirmary for a few days."

Bullen still didn't reply. Brubaker picked up a folder from the kitchen table.

"I've been studying your file. It says here you were born in Louisiana. That your twin brother was run over by a train at age fifteen when the two of you tried to run away from Hartsville Reformatory in Texas."

"They shot Hollis," Bullen said. "Then put him on the tracks so the train would hit him. To make it look like an accident. 'N' that kinda soured me, you know. So I started stealin' cars. Got me a '65 Pontiac sedan that first time. Then got arrested . . . let's see . . . for swipin' a '69 Pontiac convertible with red leather upholstery. With them big ole chrome skirts, remember?"

"You liked Pontiacs?"

"They fucked up the engine in '69. Anyhow, I got three years on that. Then come the toilet. Got arrested for vagrancy, so got put in this cell with six other guys. We broke the toilet clean off the wall. They charged me with destruction of city property over fifty dollars —another felony. Then they said that was a life sentence 'cause that was three felonies, which it wasn't. Anyhow, I got life."

"So you started escaping."

"Damn straight. Bein' in trouble inside or outside don't mean shit to me. Same diff'rence."

"You still on the shit detail?"

"Down on death row ever' day," Bullen sighed. "An' I tell you, them boys scare me some."

"I want you to be a trusty, Larry Lee, and run my

motor pool," Brubaker said. "You love cars, so I figure that's a good job for you."

Larry Lee Bullen stared a moment in silence.

"Brubaker, I been studyin' you since you rolled in, an' it come clear to me you're a weird fuckin' individual, you follow?" Bullen said. "I ain't completely figured you out either."

"That mean you'll run the motor pool?"

"Be the new warden's boy?"

"I've got to have some help."

"You got enemies," Bullen told him, stubbing out his cigarette in the kitchen sink. "I don't need 'em for my own. An' as far as your motor pool, listen, I got news for you: gimmie a car to drive an' I'll take it through them gates an' never come back. I ain't through runnin', even if Huey Rauch tells me he'll bust my back if I ever try again."

"Your answer is no, then?"

"It sure is," Bullen said, adjourning the meeting. " 'Cause the whole world's fucked up, Brubaker, and it ain't no use tryin' to change it. An' especially not inside Wakefield, where things is at their worst."

Standing apart in the kitchen, the two men stared at each other. Their philosophies were different, their backgrounds and drives too, but Brubaker knew that in this case Larry Lee Bullen—who, like Dickie Coombes, was tough in his own way apart from the powerful few—was probably telling a great truth.

9

In the last weeks of winter a baby was born in the bunk of one of the female inmates. The mother was an obese girl named Henrietta, who nobody knew was pregnant. Only an hour before the birth she had been sitting at her machine in the sewing shop. Without getting an excuse to leave her duty, she waddled past the matron into the adjoining living quarters, sat down on her bunk and delivered a nine pound girl.

For a few hours Wakefield waited to see what Brubaker would do about this curious embarrassment. At supper he stood up and made his announcement.

"I suggest," he told the men, "that those of you who know Henrietta might want to help by sending over a present or two."

"Some of us knew Henrietta real well," a voice said, and everybody laughed.

"Is she gonna get to keep the baby?" somebody else asked.

"Far as I'm concerned, sure, arrangements will be made right here at Wakefield—at least for a couple of weeks," Brubaker said.

Some of the men in the mess hall applauded.

With that announcement, the baby girl—named Thimble—became the ward of the prison population. A crib was fashioned for her in the carpentry shop. Toys and dollar bills were sent over. The women made clothes for her and took turns changing her first diapers. And Brubaker enjoyed a small season of popularity.

The popularity lasted a week—until he arranged to

collect all the barracks weapons while the men worked in the fields one day.

It was a surprise search conducted in one day's time by Brubaker himself, with Willets and three trusties—none of the prison ringleaders—helping out. They filled up their cardboard boxes with 4,129 knives, homemade guns, clubs, metal knuckles, straps, pieces of iron and trace chain.

"You ain't got ever'thing either," Eddie Caldwell offered. It was afternoon. Everyone was back from the fields. Brubaker stood in the corridor outside Barracks B with the last box in his arms.

"Maybe not," Brubaker admitted. "But this is a hell of a start. Anyway, maybe now you, Huey, and Floyd can go into business selling the kitchen spoons to the rankmen for a good profit, can't you?"

"You got that wrong. We don't want no rankman armed with anything," Caldwell told him.

"But none of you are going to pass up a chance for profit either," Brubaker said, walking on down the corridor.

"Dunno," he heard Caldwell say. "Profit is Huey's job."

Brubaker carried the box back to his office thinking of what Caldwell had said. Huey Rauch, true, was the one much more interested in prison graft; Caldwell himself preferred the raw, physical power over the rankmen; Floyd Birdwell and most of the other trusties merely wanted their pleasures, never mind power of any sort.

He was in his office considering Wakefield's power structure in this way when Birdwell shuffled over from the trusty lounge.

"Dammit," he complained, "somebody stole my sap!"

"There you stand weighing two hundred pounds telling me that you need an object to hit a man with?" Brubaker asked him.

"Dammit, it was my good sap, leather with a little knot of lead sewn into the end of it! Besides, it weren't in no barracks! Somebody pinched it outta the lounge!"

"We searched for weapons," Brubaker said simply. "Including the lounges."

"Well, hell, don't ya'll trust the trusties?"

"I trust the trusties least of all," Brubaker said, and laughed, although this didn't strike Birdwell as funny.

In late February, Lillian phoned. The governor, who hadn't been in contact with reforms at the prison for weeks, wanted to know how things were going.

"We've got bad conditions," Brubaker told her. "Improved, but still awful, if you want to know. It's a wonder we don't have a murder a week down here."

"Just don't have one right now," she said. "The governor has troubles inside his political party. He doesn't need it."

Brubaker had to bite his lip to keep from saying anything more.

In spite of all this, the winter passed in relative normalcy at Wakefield. It was when the crops were young in the fields that the sabotage occurred and that Brubaker finally, impulsively, got mad enough to do something about shantytown.

By this time the men had been issued lighter, new clothes and boots. Their days in the field had been shortened, yet because their food had been so improved they were actually stronger, working harder and more carefully, and able to accomplish as much.

But one morning Brubaker was called to the field where the young corn was beginning to show its top above the soil. An oily sheen covered everything. Slowly he walked the plowed rows. Then, stopping and bending down, he studied the ground, uprooted a single plant, and brought it back to his pickup, where Dickie Coombes and Roy Purcell waited beside the road. He offered the plant to Coombes.

"What's it smell like to you?" he asked.

"I'm a city boy," Coombes offered.

"Purcell?"

"Well," Purcell said, taking a sniff, "maybe kerosene."

"The whole damned crop," Brubaker said, his jaw growing rigid. "It's one thing for people to not like me. But *this!*"

Purcell and Coombes watched him. They had seen him determined, but never angry like this.

A few minutes later they drove along the river road, raising a plume of dust behind the Jeep. Brubaker, driving hard, saw something out of the corner of his eye as they went along. On another back road nearer the pastureland, a yellow pickup raced along.

"Who's that over there?" he asked Purcell.

"Never saw 'at truck before," Purcell answered.

Moments later Brubaker hit the brakes. Some cattle had been grazing near the road and there was a calf lying in the grass, dying. Stopping, they were about at the point where the yellow pickup had been traveling. Brubaker hopped out, vaulted over the fence and checked the animal.

"It's been shot," he called back.

"That yeller pickup had to be free-world," Roy Purcell called.

"Dammit!" Brubaker shouted to no one in particular in the field.

They started off again in the direction of the mysterious pickup, but it was no use. The road did lead them to shantytown though, and that was enough for Brubaker. By the time they drove through that street of dilapidated one-room shacks and lean-to garages, of old cars up on blocks, of tin cans and spare tires littering a hard-packed area where chickens pecked at the ground, Brubaker was ready for anything.

"You know where you at?" Dickie Coombes asked him politely.

"Yeah, I do," Brubaker said.

There seemed to be no one there. But as they stopped in the middle of shantytown's rough main street and as Brubaker stepped out boldly into the morning light, the sound of a muffled television program could be heard: a commercial, the unmistakable hard sell announcer.

"What's that?" Brubaker asked, knowing the answer.

"Don't hear nothing," Roy Purcell said, and then he contradicted himself. "And it don't sound too distinct either."

"Right here on prison property," Brubaker said, looking around. "Some damned nerve."

By this time Purcell was walking up to the shack from which the TV sounds were coming. "Howdy!" he called out. "I don't know who's in there 'n' what you're doing, but we are out here with the warden of Wakefield Prison Farm and we're probably comin' in!"

Brubaker looked at him and almost laughed.

"Well," Purcell said, "are we or aren't we?"

Brubaker clenched his fist and beat on the screen door.'"

"Maybe nobody ain't even home," Purcell said hopefully.

The sound of the television set suddenly went off. A girl's voice boomed out from inside the shack: "Fuck you, Huey, I ain't hidin' in the dark like no human insect!"

Then the door flew open. It was Pinky Newton's sister, Carol. Brubaker remembered her from his visit to the cafe when he carried the side of beef. Except now there was more of Carol to see. She wore only a khaki trusty shirt, unbuttoned at that.

"Yeah—well, what?" she managed, seeing Brubaker and Purcell and drawing the shirt together in the front.

"Good morning, ma'am!" Purcell said cheerily, like a salesman.

"Shit," Carol said, and she turned back toward the room, saying, "Get your ass over here and deal with this, Huey." With that, she went back inside the shack. Brubaker and Coombes followed her in, but

Purcell, too scared to risk that dark interior, stayed out in the sunlight.

The television set was still turned on, but the volume was off. In the soft blue light Brubaker could make out Huey Rauch sprawled on the bed. Caught, he made no immediate move to do anything.

"Well, me, I'm leavin'," Carol said.

Brubaker took a long look at the shack's furnishings. His anger still boiled in him, so that Dickie Coombes began to enjoy it. The room told its own story: television set, refrigerator, cases of beer, an electric rotisserie, plush furnishings.

"Where's your wallet at?" Carol asked Huey Rauch.

Rauch nodded at the dining table. Going over to it, Carol helped herself to a wad of cash—payment for services received. As she continued to dress herself, Brubaker walked over to the color TV and began to fine tune it. No one said anything. Dickie Coombes obliged Carol by finding her high platform shoes. She tossed Rauch's khaki shirt back at him when her cotton dress was smoothed into place.

By this time Brubaker had turned the TV off, unplugged it from the wall and picked it up. As he reached the door with it, Coombes held the screen open so that the warden could pass.

"Now, dammit, I own that thing personal," Rauch complained, but he said it knowing he couldn't do a thing.

"He mad," Coombes said with a grin to Huey Rauch. And, clearly, Brubaker was. He placed the television set into the rear of the Jeep.

"Don't worry, Coombes," Rauch said. "He'll be comin' after you next!"

Carol walked shakily along the uneven ground of shantytown's road until she reached the outskirts of the settlement. Beyond her, a large van approached. On its sides was the inscription: CORNUCOPIA WHOLESALE MARKET. As it drew alongside her, it stopped and the driver, a civilian, leaned out.

"Gimme a ride back to Pinky's," Carol said to him.

"Gotta pickup first!"

"Not today you don't wanna," she said. "We got ourselves the warden of Wakefield right in the middle of shantytown."

The driver squinted toward Brubaker and Huey's shack. Then, getting the picture, he turned the van around and opened the door for Carol. His usual delivery service to shantytown would not, he determined, go as smoothly as it always had gone.

Brubaker approached a row of six rundown garages which bore new, shiny padlocks on the chains across their doors.

"Shiny new locks," he called back to Purcell. "Now what do you suppose that means?"

"Don't ask me nothin'," Purcell yelled back.

Huey Rauch appeared at the door to his shack now, pulling his suspenders up.

"I don't imagine you've got a key for these new locks?" Brubaker called over to him. Going back to his own Jeep, Brubaker took a tire iron and went back to the garages. With a quick, angry jerk he ripped the hasp off the first garage door. The noise echoed around shantytown just as other faces—two, three, then another—appeared in the doorways of other shacks.

Inside, stacked floor to ceiling, stood the cartons of missing chili con carne.

"Now then, that'd be Captain Renfro's monthly supply, maybe," Purcell said, trying a weak cover-up. "Man took baths in 'at stuff!"

Brubaker just glared at Purcell, Rauch and the stash of chili. This was it. They all knew it.

That afternoon Brubaker burned shantytown. A brigade of rankmen loaded every prison vehicle with stolen goods and drove them back to the main building. One by one, Brubaker ripped open the garages and found shacks and storage bins packed with furniture, clothes, food and liquor. At one point, work almost stopped as Brubaker confronted Willets.

"Try to stay with me on this, Willets, will you?" he began.

"Yessir."

"The rankmen have been working sun-up until sun-set growing produce so the trusties and the warden could sell it below market value to local canneries. Then the proceeds went to buy chili and beer which could be resold to some supermarket chain, below value again, for a still bigger profit, right?"

"You think so?" Willets asked timidly.

Brubaker tore a packing slip from one of the cases.

"You signed everything in," Brubaker went on.

"Whatever Captain Renfro told me to sign," Willets corrected him.

"Not only were all of you in this for the goods, you wore the clothes and drank the booze and ate food which should've gone on the tables for the rankmen—you were in it for big profits. These bills of lading and packing slips prove everything. And they all bear your signature, Willets, so now you can sign your own severance check. Because you're fired!"

Willets stood there blinking as if he had been exposed to a good strong sunlight.

After that came the torching. Brubaker lit the first torch himself and touched it to dry grass and kindling piled around one of the shacks. The other rankmen gladly helped out. Everyone lit torches and set fires: Zaranska, Spivey, Elwood, Leonard Ning, Mr. Clarence. Larry Lee Bullen seemed to get special pleasure out of it. As the blaze danced off his sunglasses, he whipped the torch through the air and gave a rebel yell. It would mean trouble for Brubaker, they all knew, but they loved seeing the trusty power structure go up in smoke.

"It'll be dark soon," Zaranska noted at one point. "Folks gonna see this all over the area."

"Maybe that's his idea," Bullen said. "He don't give a damn."

That night, in fact, several trusties stood on the landing of the outside stairway at Wakefield watching the distant orange glow on the horizon, the burning shacks of shantytown. Dickie Coombes, Eddie Caldwell and Huey Rauch exchanged a few glances with one another.

"He's crazy," Caldwell said.

"Naw, worse," Coombes replied. "The man's dangerous."

"Either way, somebody's gotta put a bullet in his head," Caldwell said.

Inside the Wakefield kitchen rankmen stacked cases of food and soft drinks. The line of men bearing boxes stretched beyond the wire below Tower Number One. Spotlights showed the way and the tower guards were apprehensive, but the rankmen carrying goods in from shantytown seemed enthusiastic about their work.

Brubaker carried a box himself. When he met Roy Purcell in the mess hall, he thrust the box into Purcell's arms.

"What a mess! Chaos! And how the hell we gonna work purchasing without Willets?"

"Do it ourselves," Brubaker said. "Have an inmate council and a real election!"

"What a hell of an idea that is," Purcell said, shaking his head.

"What?" Brubaker snapped at him.

"What a hell of an idea," Purcell said, positive all of a sudden—having seen that Brubaker was serious.

Over in the trusty dormitory and lounge Huey Rauch and others who had been living out at shantytown moved in. They bore a few boxes which they had managed to salvage, but their place inside the Wakefield main building was uncertain—they had never lived inside the prison building itself. Disgruntled with their new lot, they searched for bunks.

"Ooo hoo!" a trusty called toward the newcomers. "Next thing you know, Brubaker goin' try turn this place into a jailhouse!"

"It ain't funny," Huey Rauch told him.

In a select corner of the dormitory, Rauch began unloading his gear and personal belongings on the bunk of a younger trusty who sat there. When the trusty complained, Rauch reached up and pulled down the man's parakeet cage made of Popsicle sticks.

"Pretty soon, ever'body's goin' to understand who runs this place again," he yelled out at everyone. "An' it ain't no Brubaker!"

10

THE game, invented by Brubaker, was called Horse-pile, but there was so much dust and yelling that no one could quite see how it worked. It was mostly a rodeo free-for-all. Rankmen and trusties played on both sides, riding horses and mules, and the rough object was to hammer a basketball back and forth across the yard with brooms. The rules, Brubaker explained, didn't prevent the forward pass, the dribble, the punch in the face, cheap shots, tripping, clotheslining, broom-sticking or any other gentlemanly gesture.

What the men liked about it best was that Brubaker himself played. Yelling and swinging his broom, he played with as much exuberance as anyone else—and proved tough. Leonard Ning, in fact, wanted to know if the warden had ever played this peculiar American game before.

"Aw sure," Elwood explained. "He keeps a bunch of brooms, horses, mules and convicts for whenever he gets in the mood. He used to play it in college. I think he wuz NCAA champ."

The basketball went high in the air. As it fell again, it landed in a clatter of broomsticks. Spivey and Elwood found themselves de-muled.

Floyd Birdwell took a roundhouse punch at the back of Brubaker's head once, but missed and fell underneath his horse. His legs wrapped around the underbelly of his mount, he yelled for help, but nobody paid any attention to him.

A great argument broke out when somebody stole

the two goalposts at one end of the field down beside
Tower Number Two.

"Now, goddammit, who's the light-fingered sonovabitch who stole the goalposts?" a trusty wanted to
know.

"In a game with no rules, that ought to be one,"
Dickie Coombes added.

"Fuck you, Dickie, we win," Spivey said.

As the game progressed—having no time outs, quarters, substitutes or adequate scorekeeping—Zaranska
began passing out his leaflets among the spectators.
His prison rank couldn't be ascertained now. He wore a
mix of prison issue and Hawaiian modern. His approach to the upcoming election, though, was strictly
Biblical.

" 'His fame was noised throughout all the country!'
Judges 6:27," Zaranska shouted, as he circulated with
his leaflets. On each one was the bold announcement,
ZARANSKA SAVES! It was his election pitch.

At the prison gate a number of visitors filtered in
with picnic baskets to watch Horsepile being played.
Watching the wives, girl friends and families of the men
enter, Larry Lee Bullen, up on the guard tower himself with the old trusty guard Billy Baylock, let out
low, meaningful whistles.

"Oh, lordy, this is nice up here. Like on top of the
world," Bullen said. He was now a trusty guard—no
longer on the shit detail of Death Row.

"This gonna wear off quick," Baylock told him.

"Oh my, lookee there!" Bullen said, spying a pretty
girl. "You know what I'd like to do, Baylock?"

"Sure, I know."

"Well, you wrong," Bullen said, pulling his shades
off his eyes. "What I'd like to do is take her to a
dance, then afterward go out somewheres for a soda
and a talk. You know, a real *talk*."

"Your mind is startin' to collapse in on itself," the
old guard told him.

Down on the field, Brubaker gave his broom to another trusty who was anxious to get into the fray.

"What're you tryin' to prove with all this?" asked Dickie Coombes, who was watching with his usual scepticism from the sidelines.

"If you have to ask the question, you won't understand the answer," Brubaker told him.

After the game the men nursed their bruises out on the new grass between the guard towers. Women sat with their skirts billowed out, while children ran through the crowd. There was fried chicken and orange drinks from the kitchen. Huey Rauch and Eddie Caldwell watched Brubaker stroll among the rankmen and newer trusties; he had clearly undermined their power, but weeks had passed and they didn't yet know what to do.

Late that afternoon Lillian Grey rummaged through Brubaker's crusty refrigerator looking for the last two beers. When she found them, she searched for clean glasses, and at last made her way out to the rear patio where Brubaker sat lost in thought. They could see the nearby women's compound, the grove of cottonwoods and the levee. The direction of the breeze brought them the sound of the river.

"You okay?" she asked, pouring him a beer.

"I'll never play Horsepile again," he moaned.

"Your kitchen looks like you've been playing it in there," she said, laughing. "You at least ought to get yourself some paper plates and cups. Or someone to look after you around here."

"That's not the kind of advice I'd expect from you," Brubaker answered, and their eyes met. It was a long, lingering look.

"I meant," she said, with a slight confusion, "one of the inmates."

"Male or female?" he went on, enjoying her slight discomfort. The exchange had suddenly become sexual and he was liking it.

"Well . . ." Her words trailed off into a nervous laugh.

"The captains who ran this place over the years didn't build this warden's house near the women's

Brubaker (Robert Redford) enters Wakefield Prison as a rankman.

Brubaker gets a first-hand look at prison abuses.

The new reform warden addresses the prisoners.

Brubaker introduces recreation into the hard lives of the rankmen.

Dickie Coombes (Yaphet Kotto), the trusty that Brubaker wants most to win over.

Lillian Grey (Jane Alexander) and John Deach (Murray Hamilton) warn Brubaker not to dig into Wakefield Prison's past.

Old Abraham (Richard Ward)
pays for his guilty conscience
with his life.

Brubaker's tenure as warden is over, but he carries the respect of the rankmen and his own integrity with him.

compound for nothing," he said, smiling. "They had housegirls. Day and night. And parceled them out, as best as I can tell, to their favorite guards."

"If I ever get in trouble and they put me here," Lillian said, recovering, "I'll put in for upstairs maid."

Their eyes locked in.

"Tell me about the roof," she said, changing the subject.

"Well, we've got an insurance policy written up by a state congressman who wanted to protect Wakefield," he said. "I've pulled a lot of interesting documents out of our files and our insurance policy is a beauty. We're covered if the Chinese attack the prison. We're covered if a volcano erupts within fifty miles. But the roof of Wakefield prison farm just isn't covered."

"So what are you going to do?"

"We've started rebuilding it ourselves."

"Good. Because the governor wants to visit the prison himself. Now's the perfect time. The rankmen are behind you, I can feel it. And the governor can actually see things changing."

"And get some nice publicity with his arms around a few inmates and around me, right?"

"That's uncalled for," she said. "Tom's not like that."

"Right now, Lillian, I need a new doctor, not the governor."

"You may be wrong. You may need the governor behind you more than anything else. Henry, believe me, there are people out there in the state who don't want this prison to change at *all*. Understand what I'm saying: you need political clout. You need Tom. And you need me doing this kind of work for you."

"There are men inside working against me, too," Brubaker said. "And do you know what would happen if I busted them to rankmen?"

"Henry, are you listening to me?"

"They'd be dead by morning. If I put them back in the barracks—some of them, like Eddie Caldwell— I'd be signing his death warrant."

"So work with them, change their attitudes," she said. "Handle the prison, if you can, and let me handle the politics—which you've got to work on too!"

"Lillian, get me a new boiler. Get me more room for these guys to sleep. I mean, can we manage to do any of this or not? Wakefield shouldn't just be a conversation up in the state capitol. We need things—physical changes which cost money—and we need them right now. I can't live with myself if we don't actually *do* things here."

"Yes, absolutely, yes, I don't disagree," she said, and she reached over and gave his hand a squeeze, reassuring him. "Look, there's a meeting of the prison board on Tuesday, our monthly dinner meeting. I want you there. They need to meet you and you need to meet them. The other board members aren't—"

"I'm not very diplomatic," he said.

"They're bringing in this expert. He'll be giving a nice little talk about prison reform."

"That's the thing about board members, Lillian! They want to talk and discuss. They never want to burn down a shantytown or buy a new boiler—"

"You come to that dinner. State your case."

"But they don't want to hear it!"

"No, of course not. They want abstract discussion. But give it a try. You've got to politic a little! You've got to try! If you believe in changing Wakefield, you can't ignore that such meetings are the way to really get things done, can you?"

"And Lillian—"

"What?"

"A permanent doctor. We need one."

"I told you, I'm getting you one!"

"But when?"

"As soon as he graduates."

"What?" Brubaker said, breaking into a laugh. "You're serious?"

"If you think it was easy finding someone who wanted to come live out here—"

"Hell, you found *me,* didn't you?" he asked, and this time they both broke into laughter.

"Well, I *did*, didn't I?" she said, and they were holding hands, their heads thrown back, laughing.

From the patio they could look out over the fields and the setting sun. The feel of summer rode around in the air. At the moment Brubaker was beginning to feel confident. Lillian was a good ally, the rankmen were beginning to understand that he meant to help, shantytown was gone and without the terrible backlash he feared, Wakefield was really changing. He knew the struggle would continue. But elections for the inmate council were going on. Working conditions had improved for the men and women. Time, he felt, might be on his side.

In the quiet evening he let his optimism take him in its spell. He even wanted to kiss Lillian. But he wouldn't. This was their best moment: laughter, the soft dusk, promises to one another. But he wouldn't kiss her, not now or ever.

11

JEROME Boyd, his big black body glistening with sweat, stood in the boiler room shouting a campaign speech over the heads of the rankmen who unloaded coal for the furnaces.

"Ya'll know me, Jerome L. Boyd!" he shouted. "I got me a sociopathic personality! I don't have no feelings for my fellow man 'cause of how my parents fucked me up! But if you elect me to 'at inmate council, I am good for a big change in character! I would deem it an honor to put my hatred for all you assholes aside and try to help you 'cause most of you—and I ain't lyin' to you—is too stupid to help yourselves!"

The men filed on by. Jerome did receive a few compliments in the barracks that night for his oratorical style.

The lounges of the trusty dorm that evening had been transformed into political arenas. Trusties, floorwalkers, barracks tenders and campaigning rankmen came and went. At times, the debates grew hot. As Larry Lee Bullen adjusted his mirrored sunglasses and watched everything, Big Wendel took the top of a desk to deliver his speech.

"I say we gotta hang together and put some men on that council that still got their heads screwed on straight!" he bellowed. "Otherwise, Brubaker gonna *use* that council to take away trusty power completely! He already took away my damn refrigerator! We already eatin' the same food as them rankmen!"

"I heard he was thinkin' about getting a *lock* for the

front door!" Dickie Coombes heckled. Everybody broke into laughter.

In the mess hall that evening the election went into full swing. Frank Zaranska perfected his mock style of preaching. He leapt upon a table dressed in a safari hat with a gold cross dangling from his neck. He wailed and pounded his fist while the rankmen below him, sitting at the tables, ate their meal.

"And Jesus came over to my bunk and he kind of like hovered there and he said, 'Yea, though I walk through the valley of the shadow of death, I will fear no evil! Because many is called, but damn few is chosen! So Frank Zaranska, take these men underneath your wing! See to it that they get subscriptions to any magazines they want in 'at hospital! And in the barracks! No matter how obscene! Because thy rod and thy staff are important!"

He got scattered applause.

Others waited their turn to address the men. Someone displayed some bunting of the American flag, so that the mess hall had a flash of convention color.

After supper Mr. Clarence gathered a tiny audience of rankmen over in one corner of his barracks. There was a radio blaring in the background, but the men listened to him closely.

"The most dangerous kind of person around here is the one with no hope," he told them. "But I'm gonna offer you hope. Put me in that inmate council and in no time you be hopin' I gonna drop dead. Because I'm tellin' you right up front: I am *corrupt*. Just like the rest of you assholes. But I am *honest* about it. So you vote for me an' you gonna know exactly what you gettin'."

It was a persuasive argument and the men broke out in both applause and laughter.

The barracks around them, though, and their own behavior told a story: there was fresh paint, new bed linens, clean floors, a new ceiling and they were busy with an election instead of worrying about crawlers, the strap and calls to the Wakefield telephone.

By the next morning they occupied a polling place beside the community television set, which had previously been Huey Rauch's down in shantytown. Duane Spivey supervised the polling, checking off names from his master list and the men strolled by the locked box.

Zaranska, taking hold of the box as if he was healing it, began to shout as he passed by.

"I feel the power! I feel the mysterious and wondrous workings within! Say hallelujah!" he cried.

Larry Lee Bullen found Brubaker in the corridor and said, "Hey, when's the liquor store openin' up? If we gonna vote, don't we get to drink afterward?"

Brubaker smiled and walked on.

The men had the morning off to vote. Out in the yard Mr. Clarence, Dickie Coombes and Fenway Park—all winners in the election by noon—worked with weights as Huey Rauch approached. He smiled with an uncharacteristic friendliness.

"Well, congratulations," he said. "I was just given the word on how you three gentlemen managed to be the only blacks on the farm elected to our council."

"What he say?" Mr. Clarence said, jiving. "This man don't talk no English language."

"Huey done sayin' how he pissed 'cause *he* didn't get elected," Fenway Park said, going along with the jive.

"I did not *run*," Huey said, incensed. "The point I'm drivin' at is this. I got people on the outside of Wakefield ready to look kindly on the man, regardless of color, who votes a certain way on that council!"

"Come by on that again?" Fenway Park requested.

"Vote right and get rewarded, that's all I'm sayin'."

"I think Huey think we gonna vote against the white men," Dickie Coombes said, pressing the weight and grinning.

"Right on," Mr. Clarence said. "Ain't we?"

Huey Rauch stood there, not exactly sure what they were saying.

"Hell, Huey, I never seen no white man till I was

ten years old," Dickie Coombes said. "It was a bunch of niggers beat shit out of me! You don't have no call comin' round asking us to help you out!"

"Lordy no," Mr. Clarence added. "We gonna let these niggers have it just like they done to us!"

"I ain't talkin' about no niggers," Rauch said.

"Now watch that what you say," Mr. Clarence told him. "Don't go usin' that word around us!"

"I'm jus' tryin' to get a fix goin'," Rauch explained.

"Man wants a racial conflict," Fenway Park said, still jiving high.

Huey Rauch could only shake his head and walk away.

By the next morning the newly elected council held its first meeting in the administration office. The rooms themselves were transformed for the occasion. Purcell's old office had been converted into a conference room with a long table and chairs, the stacks of loose papers and files had disappeared, there were new cabinets and fresh paint, and a new waiting room outside the warden's office had been created. The replacements for Willets were Duane Spivey and the young rankman who had been assaulted during Brubaker's first night in Barracks C. They moved with efficient ease. Purcell, stuck away in a new alcove near the warden's office, seemed to lack his old power over the place.

Into this area came Dickie Coombes, Larry Lee Bullen, Eddie Caldwell, Fenway Park, Frank Zaranska, Floyd Birdwell, Mr. Clarence and three other newly elected rankmen. They moved in silence until they found places for themselves around the big conference table.

Coffee and doughnuts occupied a small table at one end of the room and as Mr. Clarence passed by he hooked a donut with his little finger.

"Shit, they're there for us," Larry Lee Bullen said. "You don't have to pinch 'em."

"Taste better that way," Mr. Clarence replied, and he popped the whole doughnut into his mouth.

Soon the men were all eating doughnuts and drink-

ing coffee. They glanced around the corner into Brubaker's office, where he sat at his desk. Waiting, they
didn't say much.

"Purcell, call Lillian Grey and tell her I can't talk to
her now, but that I mean it: no doctor this afternoon,
no warden tonight. She'll understand what you mean."

The men overheard this, stirred, but still didn't begin
their meeting. At last Brubaker got up from his desk
and walked into the council room.

"What're you waiting for?"

"For you," Bullen answered.

"*You* guys are the inmate council! Go ahead. Work
things out. I'll join you in a little bit and hear what's
going on."

With that, he turned and went back to his office.

Purcell stared at the group through the glass partition which was adorned now with venetian blinds.
Catching sight of this, Zaranska reached up and
snapped the blinds shut.

Again, the inmates waited. Some of them tried to
think of the first item on the agenda. When the doughnuts were all eaten, they lit cigarettes and stared off
into space.

Once they heard Brubaker's voice getting louder
and louder on the phone again. As they eavesdropped,
he impressed them.

"That's not the way I understood it was supposed to
work," he snapped into the phone. "Lillian Grey got
authorization from the prison board to empower you
people to go out and get bids on a new boiler right
away!"

In the conference room, coffee cups were suspended
in mid-air.

"When does he get back from lunch then?" Brubaker said, his voice rising. "Then how long does his
haircut take? Then, yes, definitely! Have him call me
immediately! Today! Yes!"

In a moment the warden came back into the room
where the council sat. "Something wrong?" he asked
them.

"Don' know exactly what come first here, Mr. Brubaker," said Mr. Clarence.

"That's up to all of you. I mean, that's the point, isn't it? One man and one vote."

"An' you veto what you don't like?" Eddie Caldwell said.

"No, not right."

"Then I move we consider a movement to discuss the shitty plumbin' in all the barracks," Zaranska said. "How many say aye?"

Everyone did.

"Somebody ought to take minutes on all this," Brubaker suggested.

"Who the hell can write?" someone asked.

"Take a note, secretary," Bullen put in. "This coffee tastes like Zaranska washed his feet in it."

"Only you'd know 'at flavor, Bullen," Zaranska said.

"This a waste of time," Eddie Caldwell told everyone.

"Maybe you'd like to resign, then, Mr. Caldwell," Brubaker suggested. "I'm sure there's a replacement out there somewhere who won't mind sitting through a meeting to get a few things done."

Caldwell, silenced, stared at Brubaker.

"What we got here," Dickie Coombes added, "is democracy in all its amendments, rules and crap."

"True, that's what you've got," Brubaker told them.

As the council struggled along, Brubaker returned to his office. In the waiting area outside his door, several inmates occupied the chairs. They waited to register their complaints, tell him their special needs and just enjoy the luxury of seeing someone in authroity. Purcell leaned over a new file cabinet listening to the muffled arguments inside the council room. Duane Spivey moved from man to man in the waiting area, jotting down notes on what they wanted to see Brubaker about and making suggestions.

In the midst of all this old Abraham Cooke appeared.

"Kin I see the warden, Mr. Spivey?" he asked.

"Well, we gotta council in session, then these men here got appointments 'n' probably aren't even gonna get in today because Mr. Brubaker's got a prison board meetin' tonight he maybe needs be at."

The old black looked carefully around the newly painted and transformed office.

"I gots to see him," he told Spivey. There was something in the old lined face that told Spivey it was an important matter, but there was no way, he said, that procedure could be hurried along.

Back inside the council room smoke hung heavy in the air. Coffee cups littered the table and the men sat around, their sleeves rolled up, talking furiously. Bullen sat on the back of his chair making a strong point. Brubaker had withdrawn to a corner of the room, propped his chair against the wall and become a silent spectator.

"I say if a trusty escapes off minimum custody, then he can't *be* a trusty no more," Bullen argued.

"Well, sure, hell, but what about extenuatin' circumstances?" Birdwell argued, pleased with himself for remembering that phrase. "Like for instance a man excapes 'n' then realizes the error of his ways 'n' comes give hisself up?"

"So put 'im in the hole for ten days!" a rankman suggested.

"I go along with that," Birdwell agreed. "Then take away his visitin' priv'leges for a month when he comes out."

"I go along with that," Caldwell offered.

"Don' let him mail out no letter for two weeks either," Birdwell continued, getting into the spirit of punishment.

"Aw hell, just send 'im to his room 'n' don't let 'im watch TV for a week. Who knows where you find you ideas of criminal justice at, Birdwell, up your ass?"

"You know something, Zaranska?" Birdwell threatened.

"Yeah, I know something."

"About you mother?"

Zaranska leaped at Birdwell, but Bullen wedged in between them, separating them. Brubaker wore the slightest smile and stayed calm as the men settled down. This would be Wakefield's parliamentary procedure, he realized, but so be it.

At this point Abraham Cooke barged through the door with Purcell in pursuit. "Come on, Abraham, they got this meetin'!" Purcell yelled at the old black man. He grabbed at Abraham, but Dickie Coombes stood up, ever on guard for the rights of his race, so Purcell thought better of using force to get rid of the intruder.

"I is gonna kill myself I can't clean my conscious," Abraham said, looking at Brubaker. In the silence which followed, Brubaker stood up.

"What're you talking about, Abraham?"

Abraham Cooke stood in the doorway to the council room looking as if he might cry. His hands moved across his bib overalls. Roy Purcell stood behind him, wincing and smirking.

"Ever'body seein' the man now," Abraham said "All my years I ain't been complainin' to see the man, but I wants to tell some stuff in private that I has did."

Dickie Coombes, still feeling protective toward Abraham, came around the table. He put his arm on the old man's shoulder.

"You don't owe nobody in here no explanation 'bout nothin'," he told him. "Come on, let's go down to the barracks an' rest."

"Something just happen?" Brubaker quickly asked.

Abraham Cooke looked at Brubaker, confused. He opened his mouth to speak, but didn't.

"Has something *just* happened?" Brubaker went on.

"No sir. It tooken place a lotsa times."

"You come on into my office," Brubaker told him. "The rest of you guys can manage."

"Others out here been waitin' longer," Purcell interjected.

"Tell them a story then, Roy, okay?" Brubaker suggested, and he steered Abraham Cooke into his office and closed the door.

Purcell and Coombes stood watching with concern.

"This gonna be bad," Purcell said to no one in particular.

"Purcell, you standin' in a private meetin'. This here's not open to the public," Bullen called from the conference table.

Inside Brubaker's office Abraham Cooke sat down slowly in a chair as the warden directed him to do. Brubaker pulled the blinds on the glass partition, so that Purcell's view no longer existed, but sounds drifted in during that beginning silence: Spivey pecking away at the typewriter, the resumed debate in the conference room. On Brubaker's desk were various types of corn—products of the farm—and Abraham Cook nervously picked one up and fumbled with it.

"Go ahead, let's hear it," Brubaker said, and he reached into his file drawer—all in order, now, and adorned with colored tabs—to pull out Abraham Cooke's record. Brubaker began looking through the old man's folder. There were yellowed pages, many torn in two, several upside down.

"I first come to Wakefield before Second World War on July tenth, 1932, killin' my baby brother wif a rock," he began. "The days we made corn liquor outta this. Growed it at Camp Five pasture. We ain't got no main building them days, jus' five camps an' niggers separate. But Camp Five was where I put Jake in 'at field side all them others."

"Jake, your brother?" Brubaker asked.

"No, Jake don' be my brother. Isaac be my brother. Yard man come ask his share that money sellin' beef, but Jake he say no. Yard man punch 'im through the chest wif a skinnin' knife."

"When was that?"

"Huh?"

"What year was it?" Silence gathered between them as Abraham pondered, then seemed to trail off into an aimless pause.

"Something wrong with your eye, Mr. Cooke?" Brubaker finally asked, leaning closer and looking at a cloudy discolored mass on the old man's right eye.

"Got hit," the old man said.

"Hit in the head? With what?"

"Trace chain 'n' rope wif knots 'n' a shovel 'n' a tractor belt 'n lessee—lemmee think—a rubber hose wif lead in it."

Brubaker studied the old face. The room seemed filled with silence now, everything else far away, as if his journey to Wakefield, his very presence had come down to this. He knew what subject they were likely talking about. Of all Wakefield's legends and ghosts, there was a special one, dark and hidden, and he sensed this was what old Abraham Cooke had in him to tell about.

"You're doing time for manslaughter," Brubaker said calmly, looking into the record folder.

"Yessir, thirty-five years."

"And how long have you been in so far?" Brubaker asked, puzzled and turning a page.

"Hell, I don't know," Abraham said.

"Well, I think I do," Brubaker said, not believing what he was reading. "Thirty-eight years, six months—according to this."

Abraham Cooke's face knotted in an effort to comprehend. In the new silence the intercom on Brubaker's desk buzzed. When the warden hit a button, Purcell's voice rasped out.

"Got that new doctor Miss Grey sent!" Purcell announced, happy to interrupt what he knew was going on. "He just arrived and here he stands waitin' to say hello!"

"Great," Brubaker answered. "Tell him just a minute."

"And now what about these other guys with complaints? I send 'em back to the barracks?"

"Lotsa other guys," Abraham Cooke began again, not understanding who or what was talking. "Man says,

'Abraham, chop 'em up in lil' tiny pieces, then take 'em for a walk down in them shadows!' "

"Reschedule all the others," Brubaker said quickly into the intercom. "We'll see them tomorrow."

Purcell started to argue, but Brubaker lifted his finger off the intercom button to shut out the sound of the interfering voice.

"I give Jake's clothes to the laundry," Abraham Cooke went on. "Christmas day we stuck 'im in close to the fence where all them dead boys now was at. Must be a hundred by now."

"Are you talking about the bodies?" Brubaker asked him, leaning close. "All the men who are supposed to be buried on this farm?"

"Yessir, down by the levee."

"A lot of people talk about this, Abraham. But there's fifteen thousand acres out there, you know that, don't you?" Brubaker said.

"I knows where they layin'. Camp Five pasture."

Brubaker watched the old man, uncertain. Abraham peeled at the cornsilk on the stalk in his fingers.

"How do you know?" he asked him.

" 'Cause I was the coffin maker."

Brubaker waited, then took a deep breath.

"Will you show me where?" he asked.

Abraham nodded yes, then put his head down in his hands.

Behind Abraham's chair, the door opened and Purcell ushered in a young man, dressed in a suit, who entered nervously.

"Got the new doc right here," Purcell managed.

"Dr. Campbell?" Brubaker asked, rising and offering his hand.

"Yessir, Bruce. Call me Bruce, that's fine," the young man said and his voice cracked.

"How old are you, Bruce?" Brubaker wanted to know.

"Not very," the young man answered.

Purcell fixed Abrham Cooke with a stare, as if he

knew, but the old man didn't raise his head. His face was buried in that cornstalk and his thoughts were lost, gone in all the years, and in the dreams and knowledge he could not forget.

12

THERE was plenty to accomplish at Wakefield, Brubaker knew, without digging up one hundred bodies from the levee. If he did dig and if he found the evidence he knew was there, a scandal would erupt, he realized, and embarrass the whole state.

For a while he tried to content himself with Wakefield's peculiar craziness. The young doctor was at work in a renovated infirmary. Most of the women inmates had been paroled or sent home on furloughs. Many of his new activities were successful. Why let things erupt? Why dig? Yet he couldn't put the thought from his mind.

He sought the answer inside himself.

A normal college student, a grad student in criminology and penal service, he had never been a radical idealist. He had been fired at the Indiana prison, but not really for taking a hard line against his conservative superiors—just for talking back. But now things were different and he knew why: his experience inside the barracks, on the longline and in the mess hall of Wakefield those first weeks. He had experienced something deep in his gut. And his devotion to radical change wasn't ideological or intellectual in any way. Wakefield was his. He had suffered it and now he would change it.

And change would have to be radical. They needed new buildings here. And deeper still, a new attitude throughout the state.

If I dig on that levee where old Abraham shows me, he thought, I'll probably lose my job and all my future plans here. But let the next warden go slow, let him develop programs and institute thoughtful policies, he also argued with himself, and let me be the one who nags, scuttles the old ways, angers the politicians. Somebody has to do that. Someone has to start a revolution before any real evolution can come about.

On a Saturday morning, thinking about all this, he got up late, shaved and stood before his cracked bathroom mirror. His face, he decided, showed more age since his arrival at Wakefield.

He had just finished wiping off his chin with a towel when he heard a light tapping at his back door. Moving through the kitchen, he opened the back screen to find a young girl standing there.

"I'm Doralee," she informed him, and came up the steps and into his kitchen.

"You the one supposed to clean the house?" he asked her.

"Sort of," she said, smiling "You got any ashes you need hauled?"

They stood looking at each other. Doralee couldn't be more than sixteen, he decided at first. Dressed in the regulation khaki shirt and blouse of the women's compound, she stood first on one foot then the other as they talked.

"Who sent you over here? The matron?"

"She said you'd know what to do with me," Doralee said. She was even more suggestive than she meant to be, and she meant a great deal. She had a slim waist, large hips and breasts and a tough smile.

"Well, where's your mop and broom?" Brubaker asked her, smiling.

"Shit, honey, matron told me you'd have all the equipment," Doralee said, and she laughed out loud.

Brubaker laughed too.

"I'm glad the matron is thinking of my welfare," he told Doralee.

"A lot 'a them girls over in the sewing room thinkin' of you," Doralee said. "There ain't nothin' you got they wouldn't clean and polish for you."

"I tell you what I need," Brubaker said, in a voice filled with quiet intimacy. "And it isn't a housecleaning."

Doralee laughed out loud again. She looked around his kitchen as if she just needed available cabinet space. "Go ahead, tell me."

"You're new here, aren't you?" he asked.

"You know it. And I ain't goin' be bored either."

"Well, since you're new, maybe you can't arrange to give me what I want," he said, leading her on.

"You try me," she told him.

"Well, I want a new khaki suit. Made out of prison fabric, but with a business suit look—something special for the Wakefield warden."

"You mean sewing?"

"That's all I need."

Doralee looked at him. "Matron said you been here alone for weeks and that you might need—well, I thought—"

"What?" he asked, smiling down at her.

"Shit, I thought you might like to get rid of the clothes you got on. Never mind no new suit."

"Come on," Brubaker told her. "I'll walk you back over to the compound."

They strolled across the yard beneath the cotton-woods. Doralee's stride was a thing of beauty, but as amused as Brubaker was with her he found himself feeling a tender pity for her even more than this. She was a daughter of the backwoods, poor, down and out, and if things continued to go wrong for her at Wakefield, he knew, they would never get right.

"I ain't gonna like Wakefield if this is how it gonna be," she told him as they walked.

"You get out of here as quick as you can," he told her. "Don't worry about getting into some good times while you're here, just get out. Then you go as far from Wakefield as you can and meet yourself some-body who cares."

"There ain't none of them," she sighed.

"Oh yes, there is," he told her. "There are boys out there who'll look into those green eyes and really care."

Doralee, he noticed, was smiling big.

"Glad you noticed what color eyes I got," she said. When they were admitted to the gate of the women's compound, she took his hand in hers.

"You gonna get a nice khaki outfit from me," she said. "I cain't sew for shit, but you gonna get it eventually."

They had their last laugh as she went inside. For a moment Brubaker thought of going in and giving the matron a reprimand, but decided against it. Then, as he turned back toward the main building, he saw Purcell hurrying toward him.

What news, he wondered, does the new day bring?

"What you want first?" Purcell asked as they approached each other. "The good news or the bad news?"

"I can't wait for either one."

"Good news is a man come back to prison on his own."

"What do you mean?" Brubaker asked, as they both turned their footsteps toward the office.

"We've had so many fellers out on furlough to diff'rent farms that we forgot one. Name's Dooley Neal. He been down in Blankenship County for over a year an' ain't heard from us and we ain't heard from him. This morning he showed up. Said the place looks real nice nowadays."

"What's he been doing?"

"Workin' livestock for this farmer. But the reason he's back is the wife done taken a shine to him. I think he got told to leave before he got shot. He had no place to go but here."

"He's a trusty?"

"Aw sure. He lived out at shantytown some. Then he got assigned to C.P Woodward. Then to this farmer. Then we forgot him."

"What's the bad news?" Brubaker wanted to know.

"Bad news is that all the dog boys run off."

"Why?"

"Hell, 'cause you took away all their special priv'-leges, like they couldn't get no sirloin or beer out there at the kennels anymore an' had to come eat in the mess hall like reg'lar folks."

"Where'd they go?" Brubaker asked as they reached the main gate and passed under Tower One.

"Shit," Purcell drawled. "You know how them boys can run. They prob'ly arrived on the outskirts of Chicago by this time."

"I suppose they took the dogs?"

"They left us one litter, barely weaned," Purcell said.

"Call the troopers," Brubaker sighed as they walked down the corridor and into the office. "And, Purcell, let's try to keep this out of the papers—at least until we catch a couple of them."

"You sound like Captain Renfro," Purcell said with pride.

"It's just that we're going to have lots of publicity," Brubaker confided in him. "And I don't need the pa-pers to make big stories out of our escapes, which we have all the time."

Purcell's eyes narrowed. "We got big news comin'?" he asked.

"Maybe," Brubaker said, and he went into his office. "Get me Dooley Neal," he called back. "And tell Spivey to start lining them up in the waiting room. It's going to be a long day."

"Yessir," Purcell shouted back.

Brubaker braced himself behind his desk. He still couldn't decide about digging on the levee. He knew that Wakefield's daily traumas should be enough, but the ghosts were calling and beckoning.

He fretted over it all the next day too, which was another family day at Wakefield.

It was a warm day, summer in the air, and the fam-ilies and friends of the inmates again streamed through the gates to watch the men play Horsepile, to spread picnics on the grass and to touch their loved ones. A number of scenes made Brubaker feel particularly good; he saw a cluster of bodies, the wife, husband and three children, all hugging and giggling, out beside the wire fence. Sitting on the front steps, having a bowl of stew and cornbread, was Old Billy, the mad fisherman. He was having a conversation with Zaranska, who was telling him stories. The old man seemed to have a grin of comprehension and real joy on his face. Down at the women's compound there were lots of visitors too, and Brubaker drove over in the station wagon to pass among them, to nod and to accept a piece of fried chicken from a picnic basket.

All this while the levee was on his mind.

He couldn't decide whether to mention it when he went up to the state capitol for the prison board meeting. No, better not do that, he told himself; if I'm going to dig, I'll just dig. And let the skeletons come out.

That evening he went back over to the administration building as the families and visitors left. Still cautious, he saw that the inmates were checked for weapons as they returned to the barracks.

During the check, Purcell came up to him.

"I got Abraham Cooke's papers ready," Purcell told him. "We can prob'ly get him out of here by Tuesday."

"Good," Brubaker said. "He's had enough of Wakefield."

"What'd the old feller tell ya?" Purcell suddenly asked.

"What do you mean?"

"In the office that day. Said he had somethin' to tell ya."

"It was about his record," Brubaker lied. "He wasn't sure, but he thought he had served too much time."

Brubaker could tell by Purcell's face that the reply didn't satisfy him, but thought no more about it at the time.

13

THAT afternoon Brubaker emerged from the warden's house wearing a suit and tie. His plan was to drive up to the state capitol for the meeting of the prison board and to return late the same night. As he came out toward the station wagon, Dickie Coombes and Larry Lee Bullen stood waiting for him. Bullen was tossing rocks at the trees.

"We gonna hold the fort, don't worry," Bullen assured him. In that gray morning light with a mist lying on the fields before sun-up, Bullen still wore his dark glasses.

"I'll be back around midnight," Brubaker told them.

"I wanna know what you gonna do about Abraham," Dickie Coombes said, still looking out for his own.

"I've got Purcell filling out forms in triplicate," Brubaker answered. "He's on his way out."

"I figure you should take him up to the city with you," Coombes said. "It ain't no good for him here."

"You look after him. I'll be back tonight."

Brubaker slipped into the car and shut the door. Bullen couldn't help what he felt and said with more enthusiasm than he meant to, "Go get 'em, Henry!" Brubaker gave them a smile as he drove off. By contrast, Dickie Coombes' face was creased in worry. Clearly, his confidence in the warden wasn't as firm as Bullen's.

As the station wagon disappeared down the road, Coombes turned and started back toward the administration building. Bullen fell in behind.

That night Abraham Cooke was on his bunk at the rear of Barracks C when Roy Purcell showed up.

"What is it?" the old man wanted to know.

"Abe, boy, look sharp now and c'mon," Purcell said, and he put a hand on Abraham's shoulder and led him toward the corridor.

"What is it?" the old man insisted.

"Doc wants to see you. C'mon, you know. The new doc."

"I ain't sick," he argued.

"Just a formality. Final examination so we can get you shipped out," Purcell told him, and Eddie Caldwell, standing in the corridor with the keys, opened the elephant bars to let them outside.

Purcell turned the old man over to Caldwell, then faded away.

"I don't feel bad," Abraham told Caldwell.

"You just follow me. You got yourself a telephone call," Caldwell said, not speaking loudly enough for the old man to hear.

They went directly to the trusty store room. Abraham Cooke, not sure of procedure, looking around for the doctor, had his pants and shirt off, as instructed, when Caldwell and Huey Rauch appeared with two dry cell batteries and the old crank Wakefield telephone.

"We just gonna need a couple of quick answers from you, Abe, boy," Rauch said. "You gonna tell us quick what you said to the man. Then you can go getcha some sleep."

In the barracks several inmates noticed Abraham's empty bunk. The old man's cries were lost in the depths of the barracks.

Upstate Brubaker attended his first full meeting of the prison board at the Hilton Hotel's private dining room. A lone waitress and a black busboy hurried around, disturbing the business of the meeting, reaching over people to serve the table. Lillian Grey was there. A man named Rory Poke, who served a penal institution in another state, sat with the group as an expert. Another special guest was a state senator, Charles Hite. Off in a corner, a stenographer, her hands flying over the keyboard of a machine, recorded the proceedings.

John Deach headed the board with his usual stubbornness. From the beginning, he seemed to be interested in turning the meeting into an inquisition of Brubaker's work at Wakefield. There were two other white men, Dunfield and Rogers, a woman in her late fifties, Bea Williams, and a young black board member, Leon Edwards—who seemed, along with Lillian, to be Brubaker's only ally in the room.

Rory Poke, the expert, was holding forth. "Cap'n Brubaker is a so-called expert in penology, I know, but I think he's been outta the mainstream too long," he said. "Not that college professors don't have things to contribute, but there are thirteen states including my own that currently or in the recent past rely on the strap to control men. In Mississippi, Arkansas, Louisiana and—"

"Because others do it that way doesn't per se make it right," Leon Edwards interrupted.

"It *does*," Rory Poke argued with no particular logic. "Cuts down the time lost due to men sittin' in the hole. Gets more men out on the labor force!" As he spoke, the waitress, serving everyone, mixed up her orders. "No, honey, mine's the baked stuffed shrimps!" he said, interrupting himself.

"Oops, sorry," she drawled, and began scooting plates into place around the board members.

"Simple fact we have to face is that crop production at Wakefield is down nearly forty percent," John Deach boomed out, looking at Brubaker. "That's the fact of it. All in this last quarter since you took over!"

"But *revenues* are up twenty percent," Brubaker told him. "And if you give us a year, leave us alone, let us eat our own food, sell what we have left at a fair price on the open market, then twelve months from tonight I'll show you the first cash surplus Wakefield's ever had."

"Fine, fine," Bea Williams said in a high whine. "But all we're saying is give us some warning, Mr. Brubaker! So when you're doubling the price of corn—"

"Or just suddenly, out of the blue, canceling the prison lumber contract with a valued old customer," Mr. Rogers interrupted. "A man like our friend C.P. Woodward—"

"There was no contract," Brubaker argued. "He had a deal for slave labor. And as far as the corn goes, I'm still a dollar below fair market."

"You should've raised the price all the way," Lillian suddenly put in. "Who the hell are we still trying to be nice to?"

Deach shot Lillian a critical, unpleasant glance. He was used to running board meetings without argument or interference, but here he faced Brubaker, Lillian Grey and Leon Edwards—a black man in a business suit who spoke well, which was worse than worse.

"Just how much potential cash surplus are we talkin' about here, Mr. Brubaker," asked Mr. Dunfield in a soft, patronizing tone.

"On farm accounting alone, at least one hundred and fifty thousand," Brubaker answered.

John Deach grinned and whistled. "Dollars? Come on, now, sounds like we're gonna need some high-powered Wall Street types to come down here and help us figure out where to put it all!"

"I want to turn it back into the facility," Brubaker told them. "The place is literally falling apart. There are rats and dry rot and disease. And a boiler your own state inspectors condemned six years ago."

"I believe we did authorize bids on the new boiler, isn't that right?" Bea Williams whined.

"But nobody in purchasing will take my phone calls," Brubaker said. "And you know why? Because the lives being risked around that old boiler are just convicts' lives."

"I'm looking into the whole boiler problem," Leon Edwards said.

"Okay, while you're looking into that," Mr. Dunfield said with a soft sneer, "then look into things like assaulting a medical doctor, firing a state employee's been keepin' books on that farm for years, turnin' the place over to a bunch of inmates with fourth grade educations and things like that! You can't sit here, any of you, and tell me that an inmate council is gonna work!"

"It doesn't matter if it works," Brubaker answered him. "The point is that these guys at least have to start *thinking* that they have some responsibility over their lives. And, in the end, they *are* the ones who have to change the place, not me."

"Then why the hell we payin' you?" Mr. Rogers snapped.

"Okay, hold it," John Deach said. "The bottom line here is that you wanta make life easy for these inmates, right, Brubaker?"

"No, not at all."

"I think it is that," Deach went on. "I think you kinda like men of that sort. Maybe because they're reckless, same as you. They see somethin' they don't like, they gonna shoot it up or burn it down an' make up their own laws as they go along."

"Shantytown was a private enterprise on state property," Brubaker answered evenly.

"If we make men and women the wards of the state," Lillian Grey interrupted, "then we accept the responsibility to feed them, clothe them, give them medical attention and possibly rehabilitate them—not torture them, starve them and humiliate them!"

Brubaker began, "And it's my job to—"

"To listen to the people who pay your salary!" Mr. Rogers shouted.

"No, my job is to reform that prison. I didn't come here to work for a political party or for the governor or anybody's committee. I came to this state to reform a prison."

Senator Hite put down his fork and rose from his chair. He smiled at everyone.

"Let the record show that State Senator Charles Hite desires to make a comment," Deach said with heavy courtesy.

"Mr. Brubaker, I think you owe it to yourself to face some hard facts," the senator said. "People in this state have themselves a lot of problems getting jobs, paying rent, fighting for a good living and such. Come election time, they might vote for your prison reform thing. But they'll never want to hear of taxes being raised to support murderers and rapists. That farm wasn't *costing* anybody anything before you got your hands on it. You follow what I'm saying?"

"How about we build them convicts a golf course?" Mr. Rogers added with sarcasm. "Or a nice clubhouse. with one of them whirly hot tubs?"

"How about we build them a roof that won't come down on their heads?" Brubaker replied.

"That's enough," Deach said with an authority no one observed.

"An *insured* roof this time," Brubaker added.

Lillian shook her head in Brubaker's direction, trying to get him to keep his silence on this point, but it was too late. Leon Edwards opened the question further.

"What exactly do you mean?" he added.

"Our roof collapse wasn't covered," Brubaker answered.

"That's a little hard to believe," Edwards said.

"I *do* have insurance down at Wakefield for three haybailers and some threshing equipment and six cultivators," Brubaker said.

"Well, that sounds sensible to me to have those important farm implements insured," Deach said, looking around the table for approval of his observation. "Matter of fact, I think I approved coverage on those items personally."

"Oh, you did more than that, sir," Brubaker told him. "Your company sold those equipment policies to

Wakefield. The only problem is that we don't *have* any of those machines on the farm. They don't exist."

"What you *have* got, Mr. Brubaker, is a piss-poor attitude," Deach said, weakly defending himself. "And I don't like you, but that's beside the point."

"No, it's really not beside the point. I'm starting to ask you and others to pay for your own free ride!"

"And I'm telling you this as a favor to Lillian Grey, who, for some unknown reason, believes in you!" Deach said, his voice rising higher. "Do not come marching in here from wherever the hell she found you and presume to lecture us on how to treat our fellow man! We're all sitting here for free tonight except for you! We all got other places we could be!"

Brubaker began throwing papers into his briefcase. "Actually," he said, "so do I."

"I think we all need to calm down," Lillian Grey said.

But Brubaker was on his feet and leaving the room. After giving the others a quick glance, Lillian got up and followed him.

Hurrying along the hotel corridor, Brubaker pulled off his tie. Lillian Grey came running and calling after him.

"You'll never last pulling stunts like this," she called toward his back as he hurried on.

"What do you want to hear?" he said, wheeling toward her. They stood together inside a wide glass arcade of the hotel, busboys and maids moving by them. "I'm sorry I don't have all the right answers for them—or for you, Lillian."

"Oh, Henry, they'll pull the plug on this, they *will!* And if you're not in the system, you can't change it! So you have to give them something. Let them think they control you. That's the secret—"

"Maybe you have time for people like that, but I don't," he told her, starting to walk away again. She moved with him. "They're going to fight prison reform with all they have. The John Deaches and the god-dammed senator. And there's another group who are

obstacles too, Lillian, and they're the pseudo-reformers
—those who say the right things and play politics and
get into the newspapers, but who never get anything
done!"

"Are you talking about me?"

"I'm talking about you and anyone else who won't
fight for real change!"

They hurried out of the arcade and made their way
through a poolside cocktail party. Women in long
dresses decorated the festivity. The tinkle of glasses
and the undertow of small talk surrounded them.

"Listen, I'm fighting hard," Lillian told him. "You
saw Leon Edwards in there. You saw the color of his
skin. It took me two months to get him on that board."

"Congratulations. It took me four months to get
some antibiotics," Brubaker said, and he pushed
through the lobby and headed for the front door of the
hotel.

The warmth of a summer evening was beginning.
Gaslights adorned the driveway of the hotel and sent
out haloes of soft yellow. From a nearby pine grove the
cadences of crickets began. As Brubaker walked
straight ahead for the parking lot, Lillian, upset, still
followed after him. Couples in evening wear filed by
them, going to the cocktail party at the hotel poolside.

"You see everything from Henry Brubaker's view-
point. Everything you do is right, everything everybody else does is absurd," she argued.

As they reached the prison station wagon, Brubaker
couldn't find his keys. He put down his briefcase and
searched his pockets. Then, furious, he started pounding on the wind wing, trying to wrench it open.

"I don't know what's right or wrong. I'm only interested in what works," he told her. "But we have to
beat guys like that in there. We have to beat them
hard. And you can't play their game, you have to be
smarter and tougher—damn, I left my keys in the
car!"

Lillian opened a rear door which wasn't locked.
Without thanking her, Brubaker jumped into the back

seat, reached around and unlocked the driver's door.

"For the first time it's occurring to those prisoners that they don't have to take whatever's shoved at them," he said, breathlessly. "They have an idea, some of them, that they're still human beings. So maybe when they *do* get out they won't be murdering and raping John Deach's children!"

He jumped behind the wheel and turned the engine over. Lillian reached out for him, but didn't touch him.

"I know you're making things work inside the prison, Henry, but the problem is out here, don't you see? We have to win out here, too! We must!"

"And out here they don't want to listen to you and they don't really want to see me. They line up their own kind, senators and so-called experts. And why do you bother with them? How can you sit in rooms with people like that day after day, letting them make a fool out of you?"

Lillian withdrew her hand. His words stung now, and she pulled back from him. Her voice cracked when she spoke.

"Because sometimes you don't lose," she managed. "You have to fight for small gains out here. Little victories. And if you can't figure out how to survive out here with men like that, you're going to self-destruct! And then you'll be no use to me or yourself or to any of those men inside Wakefield! And they need you, you know they do!"

For a moment they looked at one another, then Brubaker closed his door, backed up the car and drove away.

Lillian Grey stood in the parking lot and watched the tail-lights of the old station wagon recede into the evening darkness.

14

BRUBAKER arrived back at the prison late and spent a sleepless night. He had driven back to Wakefield, thinking, with the car radio off and the wind whistling around the station wagon. The fields outside his window were bathed in moonlight, a lonely, blue, faraway shimmer. And he thought of the prison, how things had changed so much already, and what his next moves had to be.

Still uncertain, he wrapped himself in a blanket to sit in the old overstuffed chair which was almost his sole piece of living room furniture. Sitting up, staring out of the window, he had dozed off for only seconds; his mind kept turning with speculations. Once he got up, turned on the kitchen lights and tried to get some paperwork finished. Some of the men were composing writs—formal complaints addressed to judges, agencies and the governor himself. It had been a good many years since a Wakefield inmate had issued a writ, but there they were: items from Zaranska, a man named Crawley on Death Row and an unusually literate new rankman who had obviously read some state law and who quoted precedents. Writs, the wonderment of self-expression. It gave him hope that the men would not let themselves be ruled by the trace chain, trusty graft or the strap. If a man can speak up or write, in some ungrammatical scrawl, his sense of injustice, he can survive, he told himself, and for a while he sat out there in the kitchen feeling all right.

Then he went back to the chair, worried that he

should not have said those things to Deach and the others.

He thought about the levee. In the morning perhaps he would go see Abraham Cooke, drive out to old Camp Five and instruct a crew to dig.

Why, he asked himself, argue with a prison board which is so corrupt and ignorant as that one? Why go slowly, as Lillian seemed to think everyone had to do? Out there deep inside that levee—he knew it, he felt it—was dynamite which could blow the lid off Wakefield once and for all, proof that an intolerable system had flourished here.

As the gray streaks of morning slowly appeared in the eastern sky, he dozed again briefly, and by six o'clock he was up. It was then that he looked across the field toward the main building, the guard towers and the compound. Something was wrong in what he saw. Reaching over, he picked up the rifle scope, brought it to his eye and peered through it.

For a moment he couldn't make out the difference in what he was seeing. Then there it was, a body hung upside down from the flagpole.

By the time he had sprinted across the field, he began to know who it was. There was only one person who regularly took down the flag from that pole in the evenings after the longlines had assembled: Abraham Cooke. It was Abraham, he knew it. His breath almost gave out on him as he ran, forgetting to take the station wagon, forgetting everything for the moment.

He unhitched the rope and lowered the body.

As he gathered Abraham's dead body in his arms, he looked up at the guard tower. Dawn had just arrived and the tower was illuminated in the first orange rays. The trusty inside the tower seemed to withdraw into a slant of shadow. On his knees beneath the flagpole holding Abraham Cooke in his arms, Brubaker couldn't think. His anger and pain had momentarily stunned him, but after a minute he rose up and carried the body indoors.

By the time the warden reached Purcell's office, he found his clerk on the phone. Purcell was dressed in his pajamas, disheveled and confused.

"It's the tower," he told Brubaker. "They say—"

"I already know," Brubaker answered, brushing by him.

In the warden's office, Brubaker pulled up short. There on his desk sat the instrument itself—the Wakefield telephone. Dry cell batteries. The old crank mechanism. He stopped and stared at it for a moment, trying to comprehend.

Dickie Coombes ran in. His eyes were wide with what he had just learned.

"Find out why the man in the tower last night didn't report anything!" Brubaker shouted to Purcell. "Who was out there? Who was on duty?"

"The man probably—"

"Find out!" Brubaker yelled. He went over to his desk and picked up the wire leads to the dry cells.

"Camp Five," he said aloud. "He knew."

"And you had to listen to him," Dickie Coombes burst out.

"What?"

"Don' gimme any what, goddammit, 'cause I had enough guys like you all my life, dangerous men comin' in, startin' wars 'n' lettin' others fight 'em! Come in here sayin' do this and do that, sayin' be brave, sayin' come on, march with me, nigger, here, take this sign 'n' wave it around 'cause I got this whole thing figured out! Well, bullshit! 'Cause then we get our asses *killed*. Not you, *us!* You see that doncha? Never you, always *us!*"

It was an awful indictment and Brubaker couldn't reply.

"Maybe you're right," he finally managed.

It wasn't what Dickie Coombes expected. Brubaker was defenseless, confused and shaken.

The big trusty turned and left the warden's office without another word. In his rage, he ran into young

Dr. Campbell who was just arriving. Putting out a big black hand, Coombes turned him around.

"Naw, don' go in there yet," he said.

"Yeah, but I have to—"

"Not now," Coombes told him.

At his desk, slumped down in his chair, Brubaker put his hand on the crank, held both wire leads in the same hand, then gave the crank a quick turn. The electric shock numbed his forearm. His fingers burned and ached, and he realized that for a whole minute afterward he was holding his breath.

By mid-morning the digging crew was heading toward the levee and old Camp Five. They came out from the barracks by dobey wagon, truck, tractor, pickup and on foot. Brubaker, in jeans and an old denim shirt with its sleeves rolled up, looked like one of the rankmen again. But they were all determined now, and together; the trusties who usually flanked the work details with shotguns and high-powered rifles were absent; a kind of grim stubbornness held these workers as they swarmed around the levee where Brubaker directed them.

"There must be three or four acres down here where we could dig," Mr. Clarence told Brubaker. "But this do look the likely spot."

"We'll dig it all up, if we have to," Brubaker answered.

Larry Lee Bullen came up with a shovel over his shoulder. "This is the only spot where the old camp touched the levee," he said, making sure. "You just want my team to start?"

"Use your heads," Brubaker said. "Look at the ground down this line. My guess is they're right here along this old fence. Abraham said something about a fence."

Within minutes the earth had been opened up in several trenches. By noon a light mist had begun to fall and the men were grimy with black dirt, Brubaker as caked with mud as the rest of them.

In the early afternoon Huey Rauch, Eddie Caldwell and some of the other old hands came out on horseback to watch the proceedings. Their silence betrayed their discomfort with this activity, and at times they exchanged hard glances with Zaranska, Coombes, Mr. Clarence, Bullen and some of the new inmate leaders who were by this time shoulder deep in mud and continuing to dig.

"Never seen you work so hard, Bullen," Eddie Caldwell called from atop his horse, but Bullen didn't reply.

Brubaker moved from trench to trench inspecting the work.

"Not too deep," he told some of the workers. "And slow up. If I'm not mistaken, we've got a few days of digging out here."

"Ain't nothin' in this hole," Coombes agreed.

"I've got a big snack coming out mid-afternoon," Brubaker said. "With some leftovers from shantytown which we just happened to have saved!"

The men laughed and Zaranska asked, "By the way, where exactly you been storin' that stuff?' Some of us been wonderin'!"

"My secret," Brubaker said. "But if you keep digging out here you'll get it."

Toward the end of that first day the whole levee seemed opened up. Dusk was beginning to gather as Mr. Clarence drove out in the station wagon to tell Brubaker about a phone call.

"Lillian Grey," he said. "Says it's urgent."

By six o'clock Brubaker stood in his office, caked with mud, wet through his clothes, talking with Lillian on the phone.

"What have you found out there?" she asked him first thing.

"Out where?"

"You know what I'm talking about. Half the people in the state know what you're doing at Wakefield today."

"We haven't found anything yet," he said.

"Okay," she said, "can we meet tonight?"

"Sorry," he said. "I'm working. Been outdoors all day and I've got a ton of paperwork at the desk tonight."

"Brubaker, please, in the morning then," she said. "Off the farm someplace in private."

"Who told you? I'd like to know how you found out so fast."

"Brubaker, you've got enemies—real ones. That's one of the things I want to tell you! Where can we meet?"

"The auction hall," he said. "At the fairgrounds where we sell our cattle. You know the place?"

"I'll find it. What time?"

"Eight o'clock tomorrow morning," he sighed, resigned to more negotiations, more needless talk. "No, make it seven. I'll need to be back here. Can you be there at seven?"

"I'm bringing Leon Edwards and I'll be there," she said, and they said their goodbyes and hung up.

On Sunday morning Brubaker drove the prison Jeep to the auction barn. The country roads were deserted during the trip and for the first time he suffered a tinge of worry. Someone will want to kill me for this, he found himself thinking. The reforms, the end of shantytown and now the digging. Someone—maybe some trusty who will take the initiative because he imagines it will win him favor—will probably want to put a bullet in me now. Or someone on the outside might arrange it first. There were so many possibilities.

The fairgrounds, then: a few forlorn buildings in a field. When there were no midway lights and carny shows, these country showplaces looked like deserted farms. At the auction barn, he got out and looked around. Only one other car was parked there.

He entered a large, shadowed, circular room with tiers of rough benches rising around the dirt arena. There were heavy odors of manure and hay.

Two figures stood in the center of the auction floor, Lillian Grey and Leon Edwards.

As Brubaker approached them, Edwards said, "You haven't actually found anything yet, have you?"

"I will," Brubaker replied.

They didn't shake hands or greet one another. Urgency seemed to speed them into the problem at hand.

"It really doesn't matter if you've dug up anything or not," Lillian said. "The fact that you're digging is having its effect."

Before Brubaker could answer again, he heard another car pull up outside. He gave Lillian a quick glance.

"It's okay," she assured him.

To Brubaker, it wasn't okay. That small ripple of fear ran through him again. But then he saw Senator Charles Hite, looking casual in a windbreaker, entering the barn and coming toward them.

"You called him?" he asked, not sure of Lillian anymore.

"The senator called Lillian last night himself," Edwards explained, but Brubaker felt now that every effort would be made to handle him and to get him into a less controversial position.

"Let me put this just as simply as I can," the senator began, confirming Brubaker's hunch. "You've got to stop digging."

"Why?"

"Because you're salaried to run one of this country's best prisons," Hite said. "Wakefield is admittedly imperfect now—like America herself—but it's going to be a grand experiment patterned after your own concept: government of the men, for the men and by the men."

It sounded like a statement Hite would later be issuing to the newspapers. "What is this bullshit," said Brubaker.

"Now listen to what the senator's saying, Henry," Lillian urged him. "Because I think you'll agree that the senator's exhibiting uncommon foresight."

Hite's icy smile stayed intact. Brubaker had the distinct feeling that the senator didn't like standing there in that dung-smelling arena, but his face didn't show his real feelings.

"We are going to try to salvage something here today," Hite said. "We are going to work *with* you on this, Mr. Brubaker. We'll release funds, let you hire people, get you that boiler—let's sit down and draw up some plans for more barracks. And why not get yourself a couple of new tractors?"

Brubaker stared at him. "How many men are buried out there?" he asked. "You wouldn't even know, would you?"

"That field was an old paupers' graveyard when my granddaddy was alive," the senator said calmly. "It's a matter of historical record, and we'll prove that. It was never a place where prisoners were killed and buried."

Brubaker looked at Lillian. In her eyes was the absolute hope that all could be smoothed over.

"I'm talking about murder," Brubaker said. "I'm talking about withholding evidence of murder, too, if this thing isn't pursued."

"I'll tell you what else we're talking about," the senator warned. "Grave robbing's a felony in this state. You don't want to end up in your own prison again, Mr. Brubaker."

"He means it, Henry," Lillian said.

"I'm calling the governor," Brubaker said.

"The governor already knows," she said.

Brubaker stared at her and then turned to leave. Walking away from them, he found Lillian and Edwards hurrying to his side.

"No one is asking you to stop the digging," Edwards said. "We're *ordering* you. I don't like being put in a corner."

They emerged from the auction barn, Brubaker still ahead of them.

"Stay out of this, Edwards. You're just another token liberal that doesn't know shit. I was hired to reform a prison and if that means putting the whole goddam prison board behind bars then I will."

Edwards headed him off before he reached the car. "I've already *been* in prison, Brubaker. Two years in Atlanta for real, not a few weeks in disguise. So you listen to this nice token liberal for a minute because I know you got a high opinion of yourself and most of it I actually agree with. But you don't really understand the inmate mentality. And you don't understand that the asshole senator in there is ready to offer you everything you want at Wakefield. Everything you need for those prisoners."

"Somehow it's just not enough now," Brubaker told him.

"Work with us now, Henry," Lillian said, entering the argument.

"We can win! Stop digging and start thinking about the men who are alive."

"We can't cover up history," Brubaker said. "Not with lies and a manufactured history of our own. And before any real change can occur, we have to begin to tell ourselves the whole truth."

"Damn, that's not so!" Edwards argued.

"There are bodies out on that levee and I'll dig them up," Brubaker said. "Then we'll talk about the future of Wakefield—when we completely understand what it's been!"

"It was a horrible place," Lillian said, holding his arm more tightly than she knew. "An atrocity. But do we have to face that? It's in the past, gone, so do we have to face it? The senator is willing to give in—"

"I've got a prison to run," Brubaker said, getting into his car.

"Maybe you do and maybe you don't," Edwards warned him, but by this time Brubaker had turned the car around, its wheels digging at the gravel in the parking lot, and he was gone.

15

THE rain fell for two days and during all this time the men on Brubaker's digging crew kept working. The field alongside the fence row at the levee became pocked with holes and cross-hatched with trenches, but the men seemed tireless, working in the mud, helping each other, drinking coffee, digging on and on. Glenn Edward rigged lights and they worked after dark. After returning to the barracks, they slept, ate a quick breakfast, then went back to the field again.

"You guys out there diggin' for carcasses been dead 'n' rottin' for thirty years!" the trusties yelled at them at night, but they kept at the digging steadily as if by doing it they would all purge away what Wakefield had been and what it had done to each of them.

On the third day they found the first box.

"Careful now, don't mess up no evidence! Don't hurry it!" Zaranska told his team, as Brubaker and the others came running.

"Scoop it out!" Brubaker said to them. "A handful at a time, if you have to! Zaranska's right!"

They were still digging around the edges of that box when Larry Lee Bullen's team uncovered another.

They had found the place: an acre of it.

"Spivey, get over there!" Brubaker called. "Tell them to spoon it out! Go slow now!"

They found so many boxes after this that they had to turn on the work lights and move pickups and trucks into place so the headlights could help illuminate the work site.

Back at the trusty dormitory the old guard gathered to talk, trying to imagine what the discoveries meant. Huey Rauch, Roy Purcell, Eddie Caldwell, Floyd Birdwell and Big Wendel sat around the pool table.

"This entire place goin' nuts!" Wendel told them.

"The man turnin' this place upside down," Rauch agreed.

"So what we gonna do? Kill him?" Purcell asked.

"Jesus Christ, Purcell, but you are truly a dumb shit," Rauch said. "Nobody gonna do anything an' tell you about it."

"Prison board'll stop him," Birdwell speculated.

"They already tried to buy off the dumb sonovabitch," Rauch said.

As they muttered among themselves, Dickie Coombes passed by. He had come back to the main building early, the others assumed, because like them he wanted no part of the digging. But Huey Rauch read the big black's sympathies wrong.

"Look, Coombes, you got the man's ear. What's he after? Don't he know he's askin' to wake up dead? I mean, there's talk. I just can't control it."

"You the only one I ever hear talkin'," Coombes told him.

"We cannot let ever'thing fall apart because one old fool started talkin'," Rauch said, referring to Abraham Cooke. The words set Coombes on fire.

He grabbed Rauch and slammed him against the bars beside the pool table. Although Rauch looked for help, no one came to his aid. Coombes, his arms all smooth muscle from weightlifting, hoisted Rauch off his feet and choked him, grabbing up shirt, skin and a flailing arm in the powerful grip. Purcell's eyes bulged with fright. For a moment, Rauch seemed finished. Eddie Caldwell, who usually came to Rauch's aid in even the smallest matters, stood by watching.

Then Coombes dropped him and walked away.

Sitting on the floor, his legs spread out stiffly in

front, Rauch wheezed for breath. As he slowly struggled to his feet, nobody said anything.

Later Rauch found Eddie Caldwell alone beside the
soft drink machine in the lounge.

"That's it for me," he said. "Time to go."

"Why? Why now?" Caldwell asked him.

" 'Cause things is over around here. An' too many
people know who put some of them bodies in the
ground. An' that's another twenty-five years that I
don't got to waste. Not on Brubaker. Come on, you 'n'
me gonna roll."

"I'm stickin'," Caldwell said. "I'm takin' my chances
in here."

Rauch looked at his old colleague with disbelief.

"Don't you know what's gonna happen to you in
here?" he asked. "Somebody gonna stick it to you.
Some dumb ass rankman you bothered a long time
ago."

"I'm a tough ole tush hog," Caldwell said. "I been
mean, but I ain't dumb."

It was the end of a friendship.

By morning the digging crew had lined up four of
those mud-encrusted coffins in the Wakefield motor
pool. Exhausted, the men stood around and watched
the grisly proceedings as young Dr. Campbell moved
from one to another inspecting the contents. Rain continued to beat on the tin roof, encompassing them in a
sound which was eerie and forbidding.

"You men need to get cleaned up and have yourselves some sleep," Brubaker told them, but they hovered around the young doctor with grim resolve, as if
they all had to see the worst of it now.

"Skull of this one is—lying—under the right arm,"
the doctor said, working slowly.

"What's he say?" someone asked. The noise of the
rain was relentless.

"Also, both lower legs severed and stacked in—beside the knees. The legs—let's see—they've been—cut
off. Both of them. I don't know why that is," Dr.
Campbell continued.

"Probably easier to shorten the man than to lengthen the box," Brubaker said. "How long you suppose they've been in the ground?"

"Don't know," Dr. Campbell said, slowly moving aside more material inside the coffin. "I'm just not a pathologist."

"We're going to need answers. And fast. Dates of deaths and causes, if you can do it."

"Maybe if we took them to the state hospital," the doctor suggested.

"We can do it, but I want them guarded," Brubaker said. "I want nothing to happen to any of them."

Suddenly, a voice began to speak. It was one of the rankmen. He had seen enough, suffered enough, kept to himself enough and the words seemed to roll out of him.

"When I was first a rankman I run off twice until finally I got told it straight, same as others 'a you: don't run off no more or we gonna take you to the levee. They said it an' I believed it 'cause by that time I seen enough. I saw a man shotgunned in the field after he said he won't pick no more potatoes. They said there's a spinal meningitis epidemic here nine years ago, but it wasn't. They took six boys they couldn't do nothin' with an' they killed 'em over in the infirmary and we all knowed it. The doctor wrote it up like it was an epidemic. I seen a man get choked with barbed wire an' we never heard nothin' except he went to the levee. I seen a new boy beaten to death. He went to the levee. A year later I seen a man shot to death right out there behind the mess hall. They say he was escapin', but that ain't so 'cause I seen it. The trusty who shot him was Huey Rauch an' they give him a two week furlough. I seen a man beat to death with bats an' he went to the levee."

Brubaker and the others stopped and stared.

"Halfway between where you diggin' an' old Camp Seven is another ditch I could tell you about," he went on. "I saw a man dragged by a horse. He was put there. Abraham done dug his grave. An' I don't know

for sure 'bout lots of other things. I don't know for
sure that they put ole Abraham on the Wakefield telephone till he was dead, but I reckon they did." His
voice was hushed beneath the sound of the rain. "But,
shit, this beats 'em. They done quit after this. If you
never digged nothin' up, they would've kept on. But
this ends it."

"They told me too," Bullen admitted. "Hell, I was
the fuckin' escape artist an' for a time, you know,
when I lived up in St. Louis they thought I was pretty
funny. When the dog boys knocked out my teeth, shit,
they thought that was funny. Then they got tired of it
an' told me: next time, boy, you goin' to the levee. I
believed 'em too."

"It's how they run this place," the rankman went
on. "Farmers run cattle on prison land. Shantytown
was nobody's business. Machines an' farm equipment
got stole or give away. Medicine out of the goddam
infirmary got sold. Food got sold or traded off. Clothes.
I worked at a deer camp for some goddam doctors—
like I was their nigger slave. But this was the worse of
it: they couldn't make me do shit otherwise, you better know that, but they promised to take me to the
levee."

A pickup rolled in and Mr. Clarence jumped out,
ran through the pounding rain and entered the motor
pool.

"Purcell, I want you to call the newspapers this afternoon. I want them out here to photograph what
we've got—before we take anything into the state hospital," Brubaker was saying.

"Aw, sir, that gonna start a stampede," Purcell complained.

"Exactly what we want. We won't be safe now until
everything's out in the open. And the sooner the better. How many bodies do you suppose we have in that
field?"

"Two dozen or more."

"Then all of you—Zaranska, Elwood, Spivey—keep
your crews at work."

Mr. Clarence, who had come into the motor pool and had peered inside the coffins, turned to Brubaker and interrupted.

"We got a runaway vehicle," he reported. "Huey Rauch in it."

"Rauch, a runaway? Why's he running?" Brubaker asked.

"Because he's the one who killed Abraham," Coombes said.

Everyone stood in silence watching Brubaker and Coombes. "Where would he run to?" Brubaker asked.

"Prob'ly Pinky's," Larry Lee Bullen said.

"Maybe," Brubaker said.

"And I wanta go lookin' for him with you," Bullen said.

"Me too," Coombes said, looking evenly at the warden.

"Come on, then," Brubaker said.

They hurried over to the armory where Brubaker unlocked the gun case and passed out weapons and ammunition. Purcell, who was supposed to phone the state police, came back saying that the line was busy.

"Coombes, take the back road out, by the shacks, and take Zaranska and Mr. Clarence with you," Brubaker said. "Bullen, come with me. And I want Rauch *alive*. Everybody understand?"

They all nodded that they did.

16

DICKIE Coombes swerved the Jeep into the burned-out remains of shantytown with Mr. Clarence riding shotgun and Zaranska hanging on back like a tailgunner. As they arrived, they drove slowly and cautiously among those soggy streets of charred shacks and lean-to outbuildings. A ruin now, all of it, and they felt good seeing it this way.

Zaranska called out Huey Rauch's name, but got no answer.

On the far side of the settlement, Mr. Clarence jumped out and ran up to the gate. Brubaker's padlock which had closed this road had not been disturbed and there were no tire tracks in the mud.

"Nobody been this way," he called back.

"We got them deserted towers and a couple of shacks down at the bend of the river," Zaranska said. "Better check 'em."

"Then we better get to Pinky's 'cause that's where he gonna be," Coombes said, and off they went.

Meanwhile Brubaker and Bullen turned toward the junction from where they could see Pinky's Cafe Bar in the distance.

"That one of our trucks?" Brubaker asked as they approached.

"Sure is. He's here all right," Bullen answered.

They parked fifty yards from Pinky's and loaded their shotguns. Brubaker was sweating as he pushed the shells into the chamber.

"Reckon we should wait on them others?" Bullen asked quietly.

"No, let's go ahead," Brubaker said. "You keep to the front of the place and cover his truck. I'll go inside and try to talk him out."

"Ain't nobody meaner than Huey," Bullen remarked, shoving his shells into place. "You ain't gonna talk him outta nothin'."

"State police ought to be here," Brubaker said, looking down the highway in both directions. "We won't press things."

Together they started up the edge of the highway toward Pinky's. Rain had left puddles alongside the road. Off in the distance, a dog barked.

They passed a tiny house along the way. On the porch sitting in a creaking swing was an old black woman, her ancient hands trembling on her lap. As they moved by, their guns on their shoulders, her eyes widened. She noted Bullen's prison khakis.

"You boys convicts?" she called in a raspy voice.

"Yes'm," Bullen answered, too preoccupied to look up.

"I'se gonna call the laws," she said.

"Hell, ma'am, we *are* the law," Bullen told her, still not even looking in her direction.

They moved on by with nothing else said.

At Pinky's they moved quietly onto the porch and entered. Bullen stood beside the pool tables while Brubaker slowly made his way toward the bar. Out of the silence came Pinky's voice.

"Ain't open yet," he called from somewhere in the rear.

Slowly Brubaker advanced. Larry Lee Bullen stood in the open front door, so that he could cover Brubaker and yet see the Wakefield Jeep parked outside.

Carefully Brubaker entered the kitchen where Pinky stood at the chopping block table wrapping sandwiches. He stopped when he saw the warden.

"Where's Huey Rauch?" Brubaker asked.

"Who?"

"Where's your sister at, Pinky?" Bullen called from the other room. A tiny crease of confusion marked

Pinky's wide face as he tried to estimate what was going on.

"Carol?" he said, overacting slightly. "I don' know 'bout where she'd be!"

Brubaker moved around the chopping block table toward the rear of the kitchen and meat locker. He saw the door beyond.

"What's back there?" he asked.

"My house, but 'at door's locked," Pinky said. "We don't use 'at door an' haven't in years."

Brubaker started toward it, stopped and turned to Pinky.

"Open it up," he said.

"Don't have no key," Pinky protested.

"Open that damn door," Brubaker said, fixing his stare on Pinky. When Pinky saw the warden slip the safety off his shotgun, he knew he had no choice and went over to a box beside the cash register, rummaged through it and produced a key.

"This place my castle," he argued weakly. "You cain't come in here an' walk all over me. I'll call the laws."

"Call 'em," Brubaker said, taking the key from him.

"Hey, I will. This here's illegal."

Brubaker went to the connecting door, unlocked it and swung it open. A musty odor came to his nostrils. For a moment, Brubaker waited and listened before moving inside.

Larry Lee Bullen dropped off the porch and took a position at the side of the house, so that he could cover the getaway pickup, the front door and the windows which bordered the small gravel parking lot outside Pinky's establishment. The dog still barked somewhere far away. A misty rain began to fall.

Brubaker moved through those back rooms. On the bed lay an open suitcase, clothes thrown into it, as if a hasty packing had been in progress, then interrupted. The television set played to no one. Slowly, he advanced, shotgun ready. The floorboards beneath his feet creaked so much that he began weighing each step.

Beyond, there was a small living room with old chairs, doilies, tarnished brass lamps and worn rugs. Brubaker took a deep breath and held it. Then he shoved a chair through the door, letting it bang on the floor ahead of him. No response. Then he quickly moved inside.

Outside, Larry Lee Bullen heard a noise toward the back of the house. Moving cautiously, he went toward a glassed-in sunporch at the rear. As he drew alongside the windows, he saw movement inside. Then, circling the house, he came to the rear door.

Carol appeared first. Then Bullen saw that Huey Rauch was behind her, using her as a shield.

"We better talk this over," Rauch said to Bullen. "I don' bear no man ill will. You hear me, Larry Lee?"

"That's a smart idea, Huey," Bullen said. "But let her go first, okay?"

"Hey, sure," Rauch said, but his next move was a devious and deadly gesture. He shoved Carol down the short flight of back steps at Bullen. As Bullen hesitated and watched her fall, Rauch leveled a rifle at Bullen's chest.

"Aw, no, don't," Carol cried out.

Then the blast of the rifle. Caught square in the chest, Bullen was blown off his feet. He was dead when he hit the ground.

Out front, arriving just in time to hear the rifle's discharge, Zaranska, Coombes and Mr. Clarence pulled to a stop and got out of their pickup. They spread out, entering and circling the house.

Brubaker charged through the back of the house and arrived at the glassed-in sunporch.

Huey Rauch was reloading and there was no time to think. As Rauch swung around, ready to fire again, Brubaker opened up with his shotgun. The blast sent Huey Rauch flying through the wall of window panes and into the yard beside a piece of rusted lawn furniture.

It was over.

Carol screamed with hysteria as Brubaker, numbed, moved outside toward Bullen. Zaranska gave Huey Rauch's corpse a quick check.

Brubaker knelt over Bullen's body, his mirrored sunglasses broken now, the life gone out of him, his running days ended.

Brubaker could only look up into the eyes of Dickie Coombes. But there were no words left in either man.

17

ALL of Wakefield was crowded with reporters, state troopers, officials and medical experts.

In the mess hall an informal hearing was under way. In attendance were the members of the prison board, including Lillian Grey, a panel of doctors, including young Dr. Campbell, and a dozen reporters from the local, state and regional papers as well as the national wire service reporter.

The principal doctor was Dr. Ward Gregory, a little man who wore a bow tie and who spoke with a friendly, downhome drawl. He was a friend of John Deach, who questioned him.

"So you've examined *all* the remains, doctor, in what . . . a laboratory environment?" Deach asked, leading him.

"I have, yes," Dr. Gregory answered.

"And the broken bones?"

"Well, they could've been trauma. But you could also say that those self-same fractures might easily have occurred several years *after* death due to a cave-in of the grave walls."

John Deach turned and gave the reporters a big smile.

Down the hall in the warden's office, Brubaker's phone was constantly ringing, but he didn't answer it. Emptying the contents of his desk, he filled up a cardboard box. Among other items were Larry Lee Bullen's sunglasses. For a moment Brubaker hesitated, then he placed them with his things—a memento he would keep. Purcell's desk beyond the glass partition was empty, so the phone kept ringing.

It was over. The governor had relieved Brubaker of his duties and a new warden from a neighboring state was already on the premises. Rory Poke, who believed in the strap, was moving into the house over in the cottonwood grove.

When Brubaker came out of his office with his brief-case and the cardboard box filled with his personal effects, he glanced down toward the mess hall. A state trooper stood in the corridor watching the proceedings on the inside. A few reporters lingered in the corridor too, but when Brubaker heard John Deach's voice he couldn't help moving in that direction.

From inside the mess hall came young Dr. Campbell's raised voice as Brubaker approached.

"You don't have to be in practice twenty years to recognize a skull which has been violently crushed!" he told the audience.

"Son," Dr. Gregory drawled in response, "we got the forensic expert's report right here in front of us. And according to my scientific friends who are very knowledgeable in this area it's just not all that clear. You can't make claims like that, don't you see?"

Brubaker moved to the bars and looked inside. A trooper, recognizing him, stepped aside. One reporter noticed him too, and told the others, so heads began to turn.

Lillian Grey and Brubaker exchanged a look.

"So we probably got a couple of dozen or so indigent inmates buried in an old paupers' graveyard out by the levee," John Deach said to everyone. "Anything else, Dr. Gregory, you'd say is pure speculation?"

"That's right," the doctor agreed.

At this point, one of the reporters spoke up. "But paupers don't die in pieces with their heads tucked under their arms, do they, Dr. Gregory?" he asked sharply.

"See here, I'm going to put it to you that this is a board capable of questioning its own witnesses,"

Deach interrupted. "And this whole procedure could just as easily have been a *closed* hearing."

"Why do you think the governor reversed his position on Mr. Brubaker?" the reporter persisted. He was a young man with horned-rimmed glasses and a gold tooth. John Deach was getting visibly annoyed with him.

"I don't want to second guess our governor," Deach replied.

"Do you think it might serve the people of the state," the young reporter went on, "if we heard from Mr. Brubaker himself?"

"We're not here to discuss the firing of the warden," said Mr. Rogers of the prison board. "We're here to refute—er, to discuss the allegations of our young doctor here at the prison that these bodies might have been murdered before being buried out by the levee!"

Those in the room and corridor were beginning to be aware of Brubaker's presence. Not wanting to get into it, Brubaker turned and started walking away, but Deach's words stopped him.

"At this point," Deach said, "we want a decent Christian burial for these remains and we want to regain control over this institution—which our warden has relinquished."

"So we don't have any more gunfights in our streets around here!" Mr. Rogers added.

"How about it, Mr. Brubaker?" the reporter went on. "Any comment about what *you* think priorities at Wakefield should be now?"

Brubaker and Lillian Grey exchanged another glance.

"Priorities?" Brubaker said, echoing the word. "I tried to reach the governor about priorities—to give him my thoughts. But we all know what a busy man he is."

"I believe that our prison board can handle—" Bea Williams, the whiny woman board member began.

"I was going to suggest," Brubaker said, raising his voice, "that the best way in the future to prevent trouble and confusion and waste of the taxpayers' money was the next time a man got sentenced to Wakefield, just take him out back of the courthouse and shoot him."

"All right, that's enough!" John Deach said angrily.

Brubaker turned to go. Everyone in the mess hall and the corridor seemed to talk at once. Deach, in his confusion, yelled at Brubaker to come back and answer his inflammatory remarks.

"Miss Grey will explain my remarks," Brubaker called over the noise. "I think all of you in there speak the same language!"

A woman reporter followed Brubaker down the corridor. He dropped his briefcase and struggled to pick it up as she leaned down close to him.

"Is it true that the state is accusing you of grave robbing?" she asked. "Any response, Mr. Brubaker?"

She thrust a microphone into his face, but he turned and walked on.

"You want us to go bring him back?" a trooper called toward John Deach from the corridor.

"No!" Lillian Grey said, rising from her chair. "Nobody touches him!"

As Brubaker reached the far end of the long corridor, head down, walking steadily, he heard Lillian Grey's footfall behind him. He turned to see her running to catch up.

"I figured I hadn't heard the last from you," Brubaker said.

"I just want to know why you think you can always walk out?" she said.

"Because, Lillian, that's *murder* they're talking about in there, and if you condone it or cover it up, then how can you tell these men why they're locked up in here? That's why there are *prisons!* Because there are *standards*—one standard for everybody the way I see it!"

"And don't you see any options? Not one? No middle ground?"

"I don't see playing politics with the truth, no," said Brubaker.

"*No* way to compromise?"

"On strategy maybe . . . not on principle."

"That's what I . . ." She fumbled for words, exasperated. "Well, goddamit, I agree with you. I agree with that!"

"No, that's the point. You don't," he told her. They looked at each other as if they were each convinced of the other's betrayal. They held the look for a long moment. They could have been great colleagues, even more. But no longer. Brubaker ended things by walking on.

Outside the prison, his briefcase and cardboard box still in his arms, Brubaker looked up the long driveway toward the main gate and sallyport of Wakefield. In the yard below the shadow of Tower One stood more than two dozen state troopers and a number of the trusties, including Eddie Caldwell, Floyd Birdwell and Dickie Coombes. Beyond stood the entire prison population. Their gaze was directed toward a man with a bull horn who addressed them from the catwalk of Tower Two. It was Rory Poke, the new warden, and the men below him stood slumping in their usual regimental rows, their backs to Brubaker, as Poke's voice echoed throughout the area.

"The business of this prison is farming," he told them, measuring his words in the cadences of hick rhetoric. "Not digging up good pasture looking for old graveyards. What's done is done. We got ourselves enough worry *today*. Never mind dwelling on yesterday. So we all got to go back to the business at hand here. 'At's how Rory Poke gonna run this place. So let's don't waste no time understanding each other."

As Poke's voice boomed around the compound, Brubaker saw a police car moving down the road from the warden's house. It swung slowly into the compound. Brubaker, expecting it, moved across the yard to meet it.

Driving the car was state trooper Captain Gerald

Cleaves. And sitting beside him was Roy Purcell, still grinning his solicitous grin.

Brubaker walked across the driveway to meet it. He was outside the infirmary and standing near the little cluster of trusties, who said nothing to him as he said nothing to them.

Roy Purcell jumped out of the car, ever helpful.

"I'll load up them things for you, Mr. Brubaker," he said.

"It's okay. I got 'em," Brubaker replied.

Cleaves was already out of the car. He unlocked the trunk which was loaded with Brubaker's few possessions from the house.

"Got your mail for you here," Purcell went on. "And I'll take care of any loose ends, don't you worry none."

Brubaker, not bothering to answer, started to get into the car, but Dickie Coombes called out, "Hold on," so he stopped and looked up.

By this time the back rows of prisoners listening to the new warden had noticed Brubaker's departure too. Frank Zaranska, standing in the back of the crowd, turned and started moving toward Brubaker.

As Roy Purcell took his place with Eddie Caldwell and Floyd Birdwell, Dickie Coombes came toward Brubaker. A smile creased his face.

"Brubaker! I'm gettin' ready to tell you something," he said. "You were right. You were right. You were right about ever'thing you done here."

Brubaker appreciated the smile, but could not return it. He walked on, but Coombes followed him. The big trusty, ever wary, had watched Brubaker's tenure as warden from start to finish. Now, in Brubaker's last moment, Coombes had finally been won over, his natural distrust of "the man" gone.

It was Coombes who started the clapping. Zaranska standing nearby, joined in and the others followed. Then the men toward the back of the ranks began to disperse and come toward Brubaker too.

"You men in the back there, c'mere!" Rory Poke

shouted over the bull horn. "I'm talkin' to all of you! Hey, I'm gonna take names!"

Coombes and Zaranska reached the fence near the squad car which would take Brubaker away. They led the clapping now, a steady, staccato beat, a pounding rhythm. The men put everything they had into it.

Rory Poke's audience was diminishing rapidly. Brubaker turned to Cleaves and said, "Come on, let's go."

All the state troopers in the yard flipped their riot visors into place, expecting the worst.

Brubaker, sitting in the back of the car, trying to keep his own emotions under control, tried to look straight ahead as Captain Cleaves circled the car and headed toward the main gate.

"You men who don't do what I say gonna feel the strap to start off," Rory Poke called over the bull horn, but no one seemed to listen anymore. His audience was gone. They had lined the fence, so that as Brubaker passed their faces would move in review, so he could see each man who stood there clapping. And the clapping seemed to grow and pick up its own echoes; the yard shook with its defiance.

Lillian Grey and John Deach emerged from the main building, drawn outside by the noise. They stood watching, incredulous. Once Dickie Coombes, who was pounding his big hands together in heavy clapping, caught Lillian's gaze and returned his own steady, proud look.

Rory Poke, standing alone up on the catwalk, looked defeated already.

The squad car moved slowly along the fence line. The men, their faces unsmiling and hard, continued to applaud Brubaker as he went by. Up ahead, two trusties opened the main gate.

As the car passed on, leaving Wakefield, Coombes turned and went inside the main building, dividing John Deach and Lillian Grey with his big shoulders as he passed.

"Coombes, I wanta say somethin' to you," Deach

shouted, but the big black ignored him and walked on.

Lillian, shaken by the display, looked at the men in the yard. Although Brubaker was gone, they continued to clap. Their hands pounded out a fierce rhythm which seemed a thing of itself now, not only for Brubaker, but for Wakefield, for themselves, for all they had to say from their deepest pain.

EPILOGUE

WITHIN months after Henry Brubaker left Wakefield Prison Farm and began teaching again—this time in a small North Carolina college—the following had occurred:

—John Deach was indicted by a grand jury for misuse of state funds and tax fraud.

—Rory Poke was replaced as warden. The new man, who was only twenty-seven years old, once again abolished the strap and tried to put into effect some of the changes Brubaker had urged.

—The visiting day picnics were among these new institutions, but nobody played Horsepile anymore.

—The trusty system was abolished. Low-paid professional guards were hired, but within four months more than half of them had quit or had been fired for abusing prison rules or taking part in corrupt activities.

—Lillian Grey became head of a state commission on parks and heritage lands.

—Eddie Caldwell was paroled. Within six weeks after leaving Wakefield, he was killed in a bar fight in Denver, Colorado.

—Brubaker's master plan for growing food on the farm, letting the prisoners eat it, then selling the surplus for profits which would be turned back into farm operation was approved, put into effect and worked.

—Old Billy was paroled, but went back to his cabin on the river to fish and live alone as a free man.

—The dog boys, unable to adjust to life outside Wakefield, turned themselves in to the sheriff of their

home county. They were returned to the prison farm,
where they operated their kennels once more while
living in the barracks. The professional staff supervised
them as they chased after escapees.

—Purcell was paroled. He went to the state capitol,
where he had money in three bank accounts, bought
himself a new wardrobe and went to work as a middle
level executive for a firm which handled a number
of state highway contracts.

—The graves in the levee were filled up and the
area was planted with new grass.

—Construction on the maximum security facility
was started. Work on the unit, meant to replace the
old Death Row compound, was twice interrupted because of the failure of the legislature to release desig-
nated funds. After several years, the facility was finally
completed.

—The women's compound was abolished. Women
prisoners were transferred to a new program downtown at the state capitol. There was no more sewing
room. The old building, overlooking the river, became young Dr. Campbell's new infirmary.

—Floyd Birdwell lost an eye in a fight with a new
rankman when he pulled his sap and tried to disci-
pline the newcomer. The rankman was transferred
to a county jail facility in another part of the state.

—Twenty-four inmates led by Richard Daniel
Coombes and Franklin D. Zaranska brought suit
against Wakefield Prison Farm for cruel and inhuman
punishment. A U.S. district judge ruled in their
favor, accepting additional writs from both barracks
prisoners and Death Row inmates as supporting evidence, and ordered that the prison should show evidence of additional reform or should be closed.

—The governor of the state was not re-elected.

The most fascinating people and events of World War II